WHITE W1
A Yachting Romance
BY
WILLIAM BLACK,
IN THREE VOLUMES
VOL. I

WHITE WINGS:
A Yachting Romance.
CHAPTER I.
ON THE QUAY.

A murmur runs through the crowd; the various idlers grow alert; all eyes are suddenly turned to the south. And there, far away over the green headland, a small tuft of brown smoke appears, rising into the golden glow of the afternoon, and we know that by and by we shall see the great steamer with her scarlet funnels come sailing round the point. The Laird of Denny-mains assumes an air of still further importance; he pulls his frock-coat tight at the waist; he adjusts his black satin necktie; his tall, white, stiff collar seems more rigid and white than ever. He has heard of the wonderful stranger; and he knows that now she is drawing near.

Heard of her? He has heard of nothing else since ever he came to us in these northern wilds. For the mistress of this household—with all her domineering ways and her fits of majestic temper—has a love for her intimate girl-friends far passing the love of men; especially when the young ladies are obedient, and gentle, and ready to pay to her matronly dignity the compliment of a respectful awe. And this particular friend who is now coming to us: what has not the Laird heard about her during these past few days?—of her high courage, her resolute unselfishness, her splendid cheerfulness? "A singing-bird in the house," that was one of the phrases used, "in wet weather or fine." And then the enthusiastic friend muddled her metaphors somehow, and gave the puzzled Laird to understand that the presence of this young lady in a house was like having sweet-brier about the rooms. No wonder he put on his highest and stiffest collar before he marched grandly down with us to the quay.

"And does she not deserve a long holiday sir?" says the Laird's hostess to him, as together they watch for the steamer coming round the point. "Just fancy! Two months' attendance on that old woman, who was her mother's nurse. Two months in a sick-room, without a soul to break the monotony of it. And the girl living in a strange town all by herself!"

"Ay; and in such a town as Edinburgh," remarks the Laird, with great compassion. His own property lies just outside Glasgow.

"Dear me," says he, "what must a young English leddy have thought of our Scotch way of speech when she heard they poor Edinburgh bodies and their yaumering sing-song? Not that I quarrel with any people for having an accent in their way of speaking; they have that in all parts of England as well as in Scotland—in Yorkshire, and Somersetshire, and what not; and even in London itself there is a way of speech that is quite recognisable to a stranger. But I have often thought that there was less trace of accent about Glesca and the west of Scotland than in any other part; in fact, ah have often been taken for an Englishman maself."

"Indeed!" says this gentle creature standing by him; and her upturned eyes are full of an innocent belief. You would swear she was meditating on summoning instantly her boys from Epsom College that they might acquire a pure accent—or get rid of all accent—on the banks of the Clyde.

"Yes," say the Laird, with a decision almost amounting to enthusiasm, "it is a grand inheritance that we in the south of Scotland are preserving for you English people; and you know little of it. You do not know that we are preserving the English language for you as it was spoken centuries ago, and as you find it in your oldest writings. Scotticisms! Why, if ye were to read the prose of Mandeville or Wyclif, or the poetry of Robert of Brunne or Langdale, ye would find that our Scotticisms were the very pith and marrow of the English language. Ay; it is so."

The innocent eyes express such profound interest that the Laird of Denny-mains almost forgets about the coming steamer, so anxious is he to crush us with a display of his erudition.

"It is just remarkable," he says, "that your dictionaries should put down, as obsolete, words that are in common use all over the south of Scotland, where, as I say, the old Northumbrian English is preserved in its purity; and that ye should have learned people hunting up in Chaucer or Gower for the very speech that they might hear among the bits o' weans running about the Gallowgate or the Broomielaw. '*Wha's acht ye?*' you say to one of them; and you think you are talking Scotch. No, no; *acht* is only the old English for possession: isn't '*Wha's acht ye?*' shorter and pithier than '*To whom do you belong?*'

"Oh, certainly!" says the meek disciple: the recall of the boys from Surrey is obviously decided on.

"And *speir* for *inquire*; and *ferly* for *wonderful*; and *tyne* for *lose*; and *fey* for *about to die*; and *reek* for *smoke*; and *menseful* for *becoming*; and *belyre*, and *fere*, and *biggan*, and such words. Ye call them Scotch? Oh, no, ma'am; they are English; ye find them in all the old English writers; and they are the best of English too; a great deal better than the Frenchified stuff that your southern English has become."

Not for worlds would the Laird have wounded the patriotic sensitiveness of this gentle friend of his from the South; but indeed, she had surely nothing to complain of in his insisting to an Englishwoman on the value of thorough English?

"I thought," says she, demurely, "that the Scotch had a good many French words in it."

The Laird pretends not to hear: he is so deeply interested in the steamer which is now coming over the smooth waters of the bay. But, having announced that there are a great many people on board, he returns to his discourse.

"Ah'm sure of this, too," says he, "that in the matter of pronunciation the Lowland Scotch have preserved the best English—you can see that *faither*, and *twelmonth*, and *twa*, and such words are nearer the original Anglo-Saxon——"

His hearers had been taught to shudder at the phrase Anglo-Saxon—without exactly knowing why. But who could withstand the authority of the Laird? Moreover, we see relief drawing near; the steamer's paddles are throbbing in the still afternoon.

"If ye turn to *Piers the Plowman*," continues the indefatigable Denny-mains, "ye will find Langdale writing—

And a fewe Cruddes and Crayme.

Why, it is the familiar phrase of our Scotch children!—Do ye think they would say *curds*? And then, *fewe*. I am not sure, but I imagine we Scotch are only making use of old English when we make certain forms of food plural. We say 'a few broth;' we speak of porridge as 'they.' Perhaps that is a survival, too, eh?"

"Oh, yes, certainly. But please mind the ropes, sir," observes his humble pupil, careful of her master's physical safety. For at this moment the steamer is slowing into the quay; and the men have the ropes ready to fling ashore.

"Not," remarks the Laird, prudently backing away from the edge of the pier, "that I would say anything of these matters to your young English friend; certainly not. No doubt she prefers the southern English she has been accustomed to. But, bless me! just to think that she should judge of our Scotch tongue by the way they Edinburgh bodies speak!"

"It is sad, is it not?" remarks his companion—but all her attention is now fixed on the crowd of people swarming to the side of the steamer.

"And, indeed," the Laird explains, to close the subject, "it is only a hobby of mine—only a hobby. Ye may have noticed that I do not use those words in my own speech, though I value them. No, I will not force any Scotch on the young leddy. As ah say, ah have often been taken for an Englishman maself, both at home and abroad."

And now—and now—the great steamer is in at the quay; the gangways are run over; there is a thronging up the paddle-boxes; and eager faces on shore scan equally eager faces on board—each pair of eyes looking for that other pair of eyes to flash a glad recognition. And where is she—the flower of womankind—the possessor of all virtue and grace and courage—the wonder of the world? The Laird shares in our excitement. He, too, scans the crowd eagerly. He submits to be hustled by the porters; he hears nothing of the roaring of the steam; for is she not coming ashore at last? And we know—or guess—that he is looking out for some splendid creature—some Boadicea, with stately tread and imperious mien—some Jephtha's daughter, with proud death in her eyes—some Rosamond of our modern days, with a glory of loveliness on her face and hair. And we know that the master who has been lecturing us for half-an-hour on our disgraceful neglect of pure English will not shock the sensitive Southern ear by any harsh accent of the North; but will address her in beautiful and courtly strains, in tones such as Edinburgh never knew. Where is the queen of womankind, amid all this commonplace, hurrying, loquacious crowd?

Forthwith the Laird, with a quick amazement in his eyes, sees a small and insignificant person—he only catches a glimpse of a black dress and a white face—suddenly clasped round in the warm embrace of her friend. He stares for a second; and then he exclaims—apparently to himself:—

"Dear me! What a shilpit bit thing!"

Pale—slight—delicate—tiny: surely such a master of idiomatic English cannot have forgotten the existence of these words. But this is all he cries to himself, in his surprise and wonder:—

"Dear me! What a shilpit bit thing!"

CHAPTER II.
MARY AVON.

The bright, frank laugh of her face!—the friendly, unhesitating, affectionate look in those soft black eyes! He forgot all about Rosamond and Boadicea when he was presented to this "shilpit" person. And when, instead of the usual ceremony of introduction, she bravely put her hand in his, and said she had often heard of him from their common friend, he did not notice that she was rather plain. He did not even stop to consider in what degree her Southern accent might be improved by residence amongst the preservers of pure English. He was anxious to know if she was not greatly tired. He hoped the sea had been smooth as the steamer came past Easdale. And her luggage—should he look after her luggage for her?

But Miss Avon was an expert traveller, and quite competent to look after her own luggage. Even as he spoke, it was being hoisted on to the waggonette.

"You will let me drive?" says she, eying critically the two shaggy, farm-looking animals.

"Indeed I shall do nothing of the kind," says her hostess, promptly.

But there was no disappointment at all on her face as we drove away through the golden evening—by the side of the murmuring shore, past the overhanging fir-wood, up and across the high land commanding a view of the wide western seas. There was instead a look of such intense delight that we knew, however silent the lips might be, that the bird-soul was singing within. Everything charmed her—the cool, sweet air, the scent of the sea-weed, the glow on the mountains out there in the west. And as she chattered her delight to us—like a bird escaped from its prison and glad to get into the sunlight and free air again—the Laird sate mute and listened. He watched the frank, bright, expressive face. He followed and responded to her every mood—with a sort of fond paternal indulgence that almost prompted him to take her hand. When she smiled, he laughed. When she talked seriously, he looked concerned. He was entirely forgetting that she was a "shilpit bit thing;" and he would have admitted that the Southern way of speaking English—although, no doubt, fallen away from the traditions of the Northumbrian dialect—had, after all, a certain music in it that made it pleasant to the ear.

Up the hill, then, with a flourish for the last!—the dust rolling away in clouds behind us—the view over the Atlantic widening as we ascend. And here is Castle Osprey, as we have dubbed the place, with its wide open door, and its walls half hidden with tree-fuchsias, and its great rose-garden. Had Fair Rosamond herself come to Castle Osprey that evening, she could not have been waited on with greater solicitude than the Laird showed in assisting this "shilpit bit thing" to alight—though, indeed there was a slight stumble, of which no one took any notice at the time. He busied himself with her luggage quite unnecessarily. He suggested a cup of tea, though it wanted but fifteen minutes to dinner-time. He assured her that the glass was rising—which was not the case. And when she was being hurried off to her own room to prepare for dinner—by one who rules her household with a rod of iron—he had the effrontery to tell her to take her own time: dinner could wait. The man actually proposed to keep dinner waiting—in Castle Osprey.

That this was love at first sight, who could doubt? And perhaps the nimble brain of one who was at this moment hurriedly dressing in her own room—and whom nature has constituted an indefatigable matchmaker—may have been considering whether this rich old bachelor might not marry, after all. And if he were to marry, why should not he marry the young lady in whom he seemed to have taken so sudden and warm an interest? As for her: Mary Avon was now two or three-and-twenty; she was not likely to prove attractive to young men; her small fortune was scarcely worth considering; she was almost alone in the world. Older men had married younger women. The Laird had no immediate relative to inherit Denny-mains and his very substantial fortune. And would they not see plenty of each other on board the yacht?

But in her heart of hearts the schemer knew better. She knew that the romance-chapter in the Laird's life—and a bitter chapter it was—had been finished and closed and put away many and many a year ago. She knew how the great disappointment of his life had failed to sour him; how he was ready to share among friends and companions the large and generous heart that had been for a time laid at the feet of a jilt; how his keen and active interest, that might have been confined to his children and his children's children, was now devoted to a hundred things—the planting at Denny-mains, the great heresy case, the patronage of young artists, even the preservation of pure English, and what not. And that fortunate young gentleman—ostensibly his nephew—whom he had sent to Harrow and to Cambridge, who was now living a very easy life in the Middle Temple, and who would no doubt come in for Denny-mains? Well, we knew a little about that young man, too. We knew why the Laird, when he found that both the boy's father and mother were dead, adopted him, and educated him, and got him to call him uncle. He had taken under his care the son of the woman who had jilted him five-and-thirty years ago; the lad had his mother's eyes.

And now we are assembled in the drawing-room—all except the new guest; and the glow of the sunset is shining in at the open windows. The Laird is eagerly proving to us that the change from the cold east winds of Edinburgh to the warm westerly winds of the Highlands must make an immediate change in the young lady's face—and declaring that she ought to go on board the yacht at once—and asserting that the ladies' cabin on board the *White Dove* is the most beautiful little cabin he ever saw—when——

When, behold! at the open door—meeting the glow of the sunshine—appears a figure—dressed all in black velvet, plain and unadorned but for a broad belt of gold fringe that comes round the neck and crosses the bosom. And above that again is a lot of white muslin stuff, on which the small, shapely, smooth-dressed head seems gently to rest. The plain black velvet dress gives a certain importance and substantiality to the otherwise slight figure; the broad fringe of gold glints and gleams as she moves towards us; but who can even think of these things when he meets the brave glance of Mary Avon's eyes? She was humming, as she came down the stair—

O think na lang, lassie, though I gang awa;
For I'll come and see ye, in spite o' them a'.

—we might have known it was the bird-soul come among us.

Now the manner in which the Laird of Denny-mains set about capturing the affections of this innocent young thing—as he sate opposite her at dinner—would have merited severe reproof in one of less mature age; and might, indeed, have been followed by serious consequences but for the very decided manner in which Miss Avon showed that she could take care of herself. Whoever heard Mary Avon laugh would have been assured. And she did laugh a good deal; for the Laird, determined to amuse her, was relating a series of anecdotes which he called "good ones," and which seemed to have afforded great enjoyment to the people of the south of Scotland during the last century or so. There was in especial a Highland steward of a steamer about whom a vast number of these stories was told; and if the point was at times rather difficult to catch, who could fail to be tickled by the Laird's own and obvious enjoyment? "There was another good one, Miss Avon," he would say; and then the bare memory of the great facetiousness of the anecdote would break out in such half-suppressed guffaws as altogether to stop the current of the narrative. Miss Avon laughed—we could not quite tell whether it was at the Highland steward or the Laird—until the tears ran down her cheeks. Dinner was scarcely thought of. It was a disgraceful exhibition.

"There was another good one about Homesh," said the Laird, vainly endeavouring to suppress his laughter. "He came up on deck one enormously hot day, and looked ashore, and saw some cattle standing knee-deep in a pool of water. Says he—ha! ha! ha!—ho! ho! ho!—says he——says he—'*A wish a wass a stot!*—he! he! he!—ho! ho! ho!"

Of course we all laughed heartily, and Mary Avon more than any of us; but if she had gone down on her knees and sworn that she knew what the point of the story was, we should not have believed her. But the Laird was delighted. He went on with his good ones. The mythical Homesh and his idiotic adventures became portentous. The very servants could scarcely carry the dishes straight.

But in the midst of it all the Laird suddenly let his knife and fork drop on his plate, and stared. Then he quickly exclaimed—

"Bless me! lassie!"

We saw in a second what had occasioned his alarm. The girl's face had become ghastly white; and she was almost falling away from her chair when her hostess, who happened to spring to her feet first, caught her, and held her, and called for water. What could it mean? Mary Avon was not of the sighing and fainting fraternity.

And presently she came to herself—and faintly making apologies, would go from the room. It was her ankle, she murmured—with the face still white from pain. But when she tried to rise, she fell back again: the agony was too great. And so we had to carry her.

About ten minutes thereafter the mistress of the house came back to the Laird, who had been sitting by himself, in great concern.

"That girl! that girl!" she exclaims—and one might almost imagine there are tears in her eyes. "Can you fancy such a thing! She twists her ankle in getting down from the waggonette—brings back the old sprain—perhaps lames herself for life—and, in spite of the pain, sits here laughing and joking, so that she may not spoil our first evening together! Did you ever hear of such a thing! Sitting here laughing, with her ankle swelled so that I had to cut the boot off!"

"Gracious me!" says the Laird; "is it as bad as that?"

"And if she should become permanently lame—why—why——"

But was she going to make an appeal direct to the owner of Denny-mains? If the younger men were not likely to marry a lame little white-faced girl, that was none of his business. The Laird's marrying days had departed five-and-thirty years before.

However, we had to finish our dinner, somehow, in consideration to our elder guest. And then the surgeon came; and bound up the ankle hard and fast; and Miss Avon, with a thousand meek apologies for being so stupid, declared again and again that her foot would be all right in the morning, and that we must get ready to start. And when her friend assured her that this preliminary canter of the yacht might just as well be put off for a few days—until, for example, that young doctor from Edinburgh came who had been invited to go a proper cruise with us—her distress was so great that we had to promise to start next day punctually at ten. So she sent us down again to amuse the Laird.

But hark! what is this we hear just as Denny-mains is having his whisky and hot water brought in? It is a gay voice humming on the stairs—

By the margin of fair Zürich's waters.

"That girl!" cries her hostess angrily, as she jumps to her feet.

The door opens; and here is Mary Avon, with calm self-possession, making her way to a chair.

"I knew you wouldn't believe me," she says coolly, "if I did not come down. I tell you my foot is as well as may be; and Dot-and-carry-one will get down to the yacht in the morning as easily as any of you. And that last story about Homesh," she says to the Laird, with a smile in the soft black eyes that must have made his heart jump. "Really, sir, you must tell me the ending of that story; it was so stupid of me!"

"Shilpit" she may have been; but the Laird, for one, was beginning to believe that this girl had the courage and nerve of a dozen men.

CHAPTER III.
UNDER WAY.

The first eager glance out on this brilliant and beautiful morning; and behold! it is all a wonder of blue seas and blue skies that we find before us, with Lismore lying golden-green in the sunlight, and the great mountains of Mull and Morven shining with the pale etherial colours of the dawn. And what are the rhymes that are ringing through one's brain—the echo perchance of something heard far away among the islands—the islands that await our coming in the west?—

> *O land of red heather!*
> *O land of wild weather,*
> *And the cry of the waves, and the laugh of the breeze!*
> *O love, now, together*
> *Through the wind and wild weather*
> *We spread our white sails to encounter the seas!*

Up and out, laggards, now; and hoist this big red and blue and white thing up to the head of the tall pole that the lads far below may know to send the gig ashore for us! And there, on the ruffled blue waters of the bay, behold! the noble *White Dove*, with her great mainsail, and mizzen, and jib, all set and glowing in the sun; and the scarlet caps of the men are like points of fire in this fair blue picture; and the red ensign is fluttering in the light north-westerly breeze. Breakfast is hurried over; and a small person who has a passion for flowers is dashing hither and thither in the garden until she has amassed an armful of our old familiar friends—abundant roses, fuchsias, heart's-ease, various coloured columbine, and masses of southernwood to scent our floating saloon; the waggonette is at the door, to take our invalid down to the landing-slip; and the Laird has discarded his dignified costume, and appears in a shooting-coat and a vast gray wide-awake. As for Mary Avon, she is laughing, chatting, singing, here, there, and everywhere—giving us to understand that a sprained ankle is rather a pleasure than otherwise, and a great assistance in walking; until the Laird pounces upon her—as one might pounce on a butterfly—and imprisons her in the waggonette, with many a serious warning about her imprudence. There let her sing to herself as she likes—amid the wild confusion of things forgotten till the last moment and thrust upon us just as we start.

And here is the stalwart and brown-bearded Captain John—John of Skye we call him—himself come ashore in the gig, in all his splendour of blue and brass buttons; and he takes off his peaked cap to the mistress of our household—whom some of her friends call Queen Titania, because of her midge-like size—and he says to her with a smile—

"And will Mrs. ―― herself be going with us this time?"

That is Captain John's chief concern: for he has a great regard for this domineering small woman; and shows his respect for her, and his own high notions of courtesy, by invariably addressing her in the third person.

"Oh, yes, John!" says she—and she can look pleasant enough when she likes—"and this is a young friend of mine, Miss Avon, whom you have to take great care of on board."

And Captain John takes off his cap again; and is understood to tell the young lady that he will do his best, if she will excuse his not knowing much English. Then, with great care, and with some difficulty, Miss Avon is assisted down from the waggonette, and conducted along the rough little landing-slip, and helped into the stern of the shapely and shining gig. Away with her, boys! The splash of the oars is heard in the still bay; the shore recedes; the white sails seem to rise higher into the blue sky as we near the yacht; here is the black hull with its line of gold—the gangway open—the ropes ready—the white decks brilliant in the sun. We are on board at last.

"And where will Mr. ―― himself be for going?" asks John of Skye, as the men are hauling the gig up to the davits.

Mr. ―― briefly but seriously explains to the captain that, from some slight experience of the winds on this coast, he has found it of about as much use to order the tides to be changed as to settle upon any definite route. But he suggests the circumnavigation of the adjacent island of Mull as a sort of preliminary canter for a few days, until a certain notable guest shall arrive; and he would prefer going by the south, if the honourable winds will permit. Further, John of Skye is not to be afraid of a bit of sea, on account of either of those ladies; both are excellent sailors. With these somewhat vague instructions, Captain John is left to get the yacht under way; and we go below to look after the stowage of our things in the various staterooms.

And what is this violent altercation going on, in the saloon?

"I will not have a word said against my captain," says Mary Avon. "I am in love with him already. His English is perfectly correct."

This impertinent minx talking about correct English in the presence of the Laird of Denny-mains!

"Mrs. —— herself is perfectly correct; it is only politeness; it is like saying 'Your Grace' to a Duke."

But who was denying it? Surely not the imperious little woman who was arranging her flowers on the saloon table; nor yet Denny-mains, who was examining a box of variegated and recondite fishing-tackle?

"It is all very well for fine ladies to laugh at the blunders of servant maids," continues this audacious girl. "'Miss Brown presents her compliments to Miss Smith; and would you be so kind,' and so on. But don't they often make the same blunder themselves?"

Well, this was a discovery!

"Doesn't Mrs. So-and-So request the honour of the company of Mr. So-and-So or Miss So-and-So for some purpose or other; and then you find at one corner of the card '*R.S.V.P.?*' 'Answer if YOU please'!"

A painful silence prevailed. We began to reflect. Whom did she mean to charge with this deadly crime?

But her triumph makes her considerate. She will not harry us with scorn.

"It is becoming far less common now, however," she remarks. "'An answer is requested,' is much more sensible."

"It is English," says the Laird, with decision. "Surely it must be more sensible for an English person to write English. Ah never use a French word maself."

But what is the English that we hear now—called out on deck by the voice of John of Skye?

"Eachan, slack the lee topping-lift! Ay, and the tackle, too. That'll do, boys. Down with your main-tack, now!"

"Why," exclaims our sovereign mistress, who knows something of nautical matters, "we must have started!"

Then there is a tumbling up the companion-way; and lo! the land is slowly leaving us; and there is a lapping of the blue water along the side of the boat; and the white sails of the *White Dove* are filled with this gentle breeze. Deck-stools are arranged; books and field-glasses and what not scattered about; Mary Avon is helped on deck, and ensconced in a snug little camp-chair. The days of our summer idleness have begun.

And as yet these are but familiar scenes that steal slowly by—the long green island of Lismore—*Lios-mor*, the Great Garden; the dark ruins of Duart, sombre as if the shadow of nameless tragedies rested on the crumbling walls; Loch Don, with its sea-bird-haunted shallows, and Loch Speliv leading up to the awful solitudes of Glen More; then, stretching far into the wreathing clouds, the long rampart of precipices, rugged and barren and lonely, that form the eastern wall of Mull.

There is no monotony on this beautiful summer morning; the scene changes every moment, as the light breeze bears us away to the south. For there is the Sheep Island; and Garveloch—which is the rough island; and Eilean-na naomha—which is the island of the Saints. But what are these to the small transparent cloud resting on the horizon?—smaller than any man's hand. The day is still; and the seas are smooth: cannot we hear the mermaiden singing on the far shores of Colonsay?

"Colonsay!" exclaims the Laird, seizing a field-glass. "Dear me! Is that Colonsay? And they telled me that Tom Galbraith was going there this very year."

The piece of news fails to startle us altogether; though we have heard the Laird speak of Mr. Galbraith before.

"Ay," says he, "the world will know something o' Colonsay when Tom Galbraith gets there."

"Whom did you say?" Miss Avon asks.

"Why, Galbraith!" says he. "Tom Galbraith!"

The Laird stares in amazement. Is it possible she has not heard of Tom Galbraith? And she herself an artist; and coming direct from Edinburgh, where she has been living for two whole months!

"Gracious me!" says the Laird. "Ye do not say ye have never heard of Galbraith—he's an Academeecian!—a Scottish Academeecian!"

"Oh, yes; no doubt," she says, rather bewildered.

"There is no one living has had such an influence on our Scotch school of painters as Galbraith—a man of great abeelity—a man of great and uncommon abeelity—he is one of the most famous landscape painters of our day——"

"I scarcely met any one in Edinburgh," she pleads.

"But in London—in London!" exclaims the astonished Laird. "Do ye mean to say you never heard o' Tom Galbraith?"

"I—I think not," she confesses. "I—I don't remember his name in the Academy catalogue——"

"The Royal Academy!" cries the Laird, with scorn. "No, no! Ye need not expect that. The English Academy is afraid of the Scotchmen: their pictures are too strong: you do not put good honest whisky beside small beer. I say the English Academy is afraid of the Scotch school——"

But flesh and blood can stand this no longer: we shall not have Mary Avon trampled upon.

"Look here, Denny-mains: we always thought there was a Scotchman or two in the Royal Academy itself—and quite capable of holding their own there, too. Why, the President of the Academy is a Scotchman! And as for the Academy exhibition, the very walls are smothered with Scotch hills, Scotch spates, Scotch peasants, to say nothing of the thousand herring-smacks of Tarbert."

"I tell ye they are afraid of Tom Galbraith; they will not exhibit one of his pictures," says the Laird, stubbornly; and here the discussion is closed; for Master Fred tinkles his bell below, and we have to go down for luncheon.

It was most unfair of the wind to take advantage of our absence, and to sneak off, leaving us in a dead calm. It was all very well, when we came on deck again, to watch the terns darting about in their swallow-like fashion, and swooping down to seize a fish; and the strings of sea-pyots whirring by, with their scarlet beaks and legs; and the sudden shimmer and hissing of a part of the blue plain, where a shoal of mackerel had come to the surface; but where were we, now in the open Atlantic, to pass the night? We relinquished the doubling of the Ross of Mull; we should have been content—more than content, for the sake of auld lang syne—to have put into Carsaig; we were beginning even to have ignominious thoughts of Loch Buy. And yet we let the golden evening draw on with comparative resignation; and we watched the colour gathering in the west, and the Atlantic taking darker hues, and a ruddy tinge beginning to tell on the seamed ridges of Garveloch and the isle of Saints. When the wind sprung up again—it had backed to due west, and we had to beat against it with a series of long tacks, that took us down within sight of Islay and back to Mull apparently all for nothing—we were deeply engaged in prophesying all manner of things to be achieved by one Angus Sutherland, an old friend of ours, though yet a young man enough.

"Just fancy, sir!" says our hostess to the Laird—the Laird, by the way, does not seem so enthusiastic as the rest of us, when he hears that this hero of modern days is about to join our party. "What he has done beats all that I ever heard about Scotch University students; and you know what some of them have accomplished in the face of difficulties. His father is a minister in some small place in Banffshire; perhaps he has 200*l.* a year at the outside. This son of his has not cost him a farthing for either his maintenance or his education, since he was fourteen; he took bursaries, scholarships, I don't know what, when he was a mere lad; supported himself and travelled all over Europe—but I think it was at Leipsic and at Vienna he studied longest; and the papers he has written—the lectures—and the correspondence with all the great scientific people—when they made him a Fellow, all he said was, 'I wish my mother was alive.'"

This was rather an incoherent and jumbled account of a young man's career.

"A Fellow of what?" says the Laird.

"A Fellow of the Royal Society! They made him a Fellow of the Royal Society last year! And he is only seven-and-twenty! I do believe he was not over one-and-twenty when he took his degree at Edinburgh. And then—and then—there is really nothing that he doesn't know: is there, Mary?"

This sudden appeal causes Mary Avon to flush slightly; but she says demurely, looking down—

"Of course I don't know anything that he doesn't know."

"Hm!" says the Laird, who does not seem over pleased. "I have observed that young men who are too brilliant at the first, seldom come to much afterwards. Has he gained anything substantial? Has he a good practice? Does he keep his carriage yet?"

"No, no!" says our hostess, with a fine contempt for such things. "He has a higher ambition than that. His practice is almost nothing. He prefers to sacrifice that in the meantime. But his reputation—among the scientific—why—why, it is European!"

"Hm!" says the Laird. "I have sometimes seen that persons who gave themselves up to erudeetion, lost the character of human beings altogether. They become scientific machines. The world is just made up of books for them—and lectures—they would not give a halfpenny to a beggar for fear of poleetical economy——."

"Oh, how can you say such a thing of Angus Sutherland!" says she—though he has said no such thing of Angus Sutherland. "Why, here is this girl who goes to Edinburgh—all by herself—to nurse an old woman in her last illness; and as Angus Sutherland is in Edinburgh on some business—connected with the University, I believe—I ask him to call on her and see if he can give her any advice. What does he do? He stops in Edinburgh two months—editing that scientific magazine there instead of in London—and all because he has taken an interest in the old woman and thinks that Mary should not have the whole responsibility on her shoulders. Is that like a scientific machine?"

"No," says the Laird, with a certain calm grandeur; "you do not often find young men doing that for the sake of an old woman." But of course we don't know what he means.

"And I am so glad he is coming to us!" she says, with real delight in her face. "We shall take him away from his microscopes, and his societies, and all that. Oh, and he is such a delightful companion—so simple, and natural, and straightforward! Don't you think so, Mary?"

Mary Avon is understood to assent: she does not say much—she is so deeply interested in a couple of porpoises that appear from time to time on the smooth plain on the sea.

"I am sure a long holiday would do him a world of good," says this eager hostess; "but that is too much to expect. He is always too busy. I think he has got to go over to Italy soon, about some exhibition of surgical instruments, or something of that sort."

We had plenty of further talk about Dr. Sutherland, and of the wonderful future that lay before him, that evening before we finally put into Loch Buy. And there we dined; and after dinner we found the wan, clear twilight filling the northern heavens, over the black range of mountains, and throwing a silver glare on the smooth sea around us. We could have read on deck at eleven at night——had that been necessary; but Mary Avon was humming snatches of songs to us, and the Laird was discoursing of the wonderful influence exerted on Scotch landscape-art by Tom Galbraith. Then in the south the yellow moon rose; and a golden lane of light lay on the sea, from the horizon across to the side of the yacht; and there was a strange glory on the decks and on the tall, smooth masts. The peace of that night!—the soft air, the silence, the dreamy lapping of the water!

"And whatever lies before Angus Sutherland," says one of us—"whether a baronetcy, or a big fortune, or marriage with an Italian princess—he won't find anything better than sailing in the *White Dove* among the western islands."

CHAPTER IV.
A MESSAGE.

What fierce commotion is this that awakes us in the morning—what pandemonium broken loose of wild storm-sounds—with the stately *White Dove*, ordinarily the most sedate and gentle of her sex, apparently gone mad, and flinging herself about as if bent on somersaults? When one clambers up the companion-way, clinging hard, and puts one's head out into the gale, behold! there is not a trace of land visible anywhere—nothing but whirling clouds of mist and rain; and mountain-masses of waves that toss the *White Dove* about as if she were a plaything; and decks all running wet with the driven spray. John of Skye, clad from head to heel in black oilskins—and at one moment up in the clouds, the next moment descending into the great trough of the sea—hangs on to the rope that is twisted round the tiller; and laughs a good-morning; and shakes the salt water from his shaggy eyebrows and beard.

"Hallo! John—where on earth have we got to?"

"Ay, ay, sir."

"I say WHERE ARE WE?" is shouted, for the roar of the rushing Atlantic in deafening.

"'Deed I not think we are far from Loch Buy," says John of Skye, grimly. "The wind is dead ahead of us—ay, shist dead ahead!"

"What made you come out against a headwind then?"

"When we cam' out," says John—picking his English, "the wind will be from the norse—ay, a fine light breeze from the norse. And will Mr. —— himself be for going on now? it is a ferry bad sea for the leddies—a ferry coorse sea."

But it appears that this conversation—bawled aloud—has been overheard. There are voices from below. The skylight of the ladies' cabin is partly open.

"Don't mind us," calls Mary Avon. "Go on by all means!"

The other voice calls—

"Why can't you keep this fool of a boat straight? Ask him when we shall be into the Sound of Iona."

One might as well ask him when we shall be into the Sound of Jericho or Jerusalem. With half a gale of wind right in our teeth, and with the heavy Atlantic swell running, we might labour here all day—and all the night too—without getting round the Ross of Mull. There is nothing for it but to turn and run, that we may have our breakfast in peace. Let her away, then, you brave John of Skye!—slack out the main-sheet, and give her plenty of it, too: then at the same moment Sandy from Islay perceives that a haul at the weather topping-lift will clear the boom from the davits; and now—and now, good Master Fred—our much-esteemed and shifty Friedrich d'or—if you will but lay the cloth on the table, we will help you to steady the dancing phantasmagoria of plates and forks!

"Dear me!" says the Laird, when we are assembled together, "it has been an awful night!"

"Oh, I hope you have not been ill!" says his hostess, with a quick concern in the soft, clear eyes.

He does not look as if he had suffered much. He is contentedly chipping an egg; and withal keeping an eye on the things near him, for the *White Dove*, still plunging a good deal, threatens at times to make of everything on the table a movable feast.

"Oh, no, ma'am, not ill," he says. "But at my time of life, ye see, one is not as light in weight as one used to be; and the way I was flung about in that cabin last night was just extraordinary. When I was trying to put on my boots this morning, I am sure I resembled nothing so much as a pea in a bladder—indeed it was so—I was knocked about like a pea in a bladder."

Of course we expressed great sympathy, and assured him that the *White Dove*—famed all along this coast for her sober and steady-going behaviour—would never act so any more.

"However," said he thoughtfully, "the wakefulness of the night is often of use to people. Yes, I have come to a decision."

We were somewhat alarmed: was he going to leave us merely because of this bit of tossing?

"I dare say ye know, ma'am," says he slowly, "that I am one of the Commissioners of the Burgh of Strathgovan. It is a posection of grave responsibility. This very question now—

about our getting a steam fire-engine—has been weighing on my mind for many a day. Well, I have decided I will no longer oppose it. They may have the steam fire-engine as far as I am concerned."

We felt greatly relieved.

"Yes," continued the Laird, solemnly, "I think I am doing my duty in this matter as a public man should—laying aside his personal prejudice. But the cost of it! Do ye know that we shall want bigger nozzles to all the fire-plugs?"

Matters were looking grave again.

"However," said the Laird cheerfully—for he would not depress us too much, "it may all turn out for the best; and I will telegraph my decision to Strathgovan as soon as ever the storm allows us to reach a port."

The storm, indeed! When we scramble up on deck again, we find that it is only a brisk sailing breeze we have; and the *White Dove* is bowling merrily along, flinging high the white spray from her bows. And then we begin to see that, despite those driving mists around us, there is really a fine clear summer day shining far above this twopenny-halfpenny tempest. The whirling mists break here and there; and we catch glimpses of a placid blue sky, flecked with lines of motionless cirrhus cloud. The breaks increase; floods of sunshine fall on the gleaming decks; clearer and clearer become the vast precipices of southern Mull; and then, when we get well to the lee of Eilean-straid-ean, behold! the blue seas around us once more; and the blue skies overhead; and the red ensign fluttering in the summer breeze. No wonder that Mary Avon sings her delight—as a linnet sings after the rain; and, though the song is not meant for us at all, but is really hummed to herself as she clings on to the shrouds and watches the flashing and dipping of the white-winged gulls, we know that it is all about a jolly young waterman. The audacious creature: John of Skye has a wife and four children.

Too quickly indeed does the fair summer day go by—as we pass the old familiar Duart and begin to beat up the Sound of Mull against a fine light sailing breeze. By the time we have reached Ardtornish, the Laird has acquired some vague notion as to how the gaff topsail is set. Opposite the dark-green woods of Funeray, he tells us of the extraordinary faculty possessed by Tom Galbraith of representing the texture of foliage. At Salen we have Master Fred's bell summoning us down to lunch; and thereafter, on deck, coffee, draughts, crochet, and a profoundly interesting description of some of the knotty points in the great Semple heresy case. And here again, as we bear away over almost to the mouth of Loch Sunart, is the open Atlantic—of a breezy grey under the lemon-colour and silver of the calm evening sky. What is the use of going on against this contrary wind, and missing, in the darkness of the night, all the wonders of the western islands that the Laird is anxious to see? We resolve to run into Tobermory; and by and by we find ourselves under the shadow of the wooded rocks, with the little white town shining along the semicircle of the bay. And very cleverly indeed does John of Skye cut in among the various craft—showing off a little bit, perhaps—until the *White Dove* is brought up to the wind, and the great anchor-cable goes out with a roar.

Now it was by the merest accident that we got at Tobermory a telegram that had been forwarded that very day to meet us on our return voyage. There was no need for any one to go ashore, for we were scarcely in port before a most praiseworthy gentleman was so kind as to send us on board a consignment of fresh flowers, vegetables, milk, eggs, and so forth—the very things that become of inestimable value to yachting people. However, we had two women on board; and of course—despite a certain bandaged ankle—they must needs go shopping. And Mary Avon, when we got ashore, would buy some tobacco for her favourite Captain John; and went into the post-office for that purpose, and was having the black stuff measured out by the yard when some mention was made of the *White Dove*. Then a question was asked; there was a telegram; it was handed to Miss Avon, who opened it and read it.

"Oh!" said she, looking rather concerned; and then she regarded her friend with some little hesitation.

"It is my uncle," she says; "he wants to see me on very urgent business. He is—coming—to see me—the day after to-morrow."

Blank consternation followed this announcement. This person, even though he was Mary Avon's sole surviving relative, was quite intolerable to us. East Wind we had called him

11

in secret, on the few occasions on which he had darkened our doors. And just as we were making up our happy family party—with the Laird, and Mary, and Angus Sutherland—to sail away to the far Hebrides, here was this insufferable creature—with his raucous voice, his washed-out eyes, his pink face, his uneasy manner, and general groom or butler-like appearance—thrusting himself on us!

"Well, you know, Mary," says her hostess—entirely concealing her dismay in her anxious politeness—"we shall almost certainly be home by the day after to-morrow, if we get any wind at all. So you had better telegraph to your uncle to come on to Castle Osprey, and to wait for you if you are not there; we cannot be much longer than that. And Angus Sutherland will be there; he will keep him company until we arrive."

So that was done, and we went on board again—one of us meanwhile vowing to himself that ere ever Mr. Frederick Smethurst set sail with us on board the *White Dove*, a rifle-bullet through her hull would send that gallant vessel to the lobsters.

Now what do you think our Mary Avon set to work to do—all during this beautiful summer evening, as we sat on deck and eyed curiously the other craft in the bay, or watched the firs grow dark against the silver-yellow twilight? We could not at first make out what she was driving at. Her occupation in the world, so far as she had any—beyond being the pleasantest of companions and the faithfullest of friends—was the painting of landscapes in oil, not the construction of Frankenstein monsters. But here she begins by declaring to us that there is one type of character that has never been described by any satirist, or dramatist, or fictionist—a common type, too, though only becoming pronounced in rare instances. It is the moral Tartuffe, she declares—the person who is through and through a hypocrite, not to cloak evil doings, but only that his eager love of approbation may be gratified. Look now how this creature of diseased vanity, of plausible manners, of pretentious humbug, rises out of the smoke like the figure summoned by a wizard's wand! As she gives us little touches here and there of the ways of this professor of bonhomie—this bundle of affectations—we begin to prefer the most diabolical villainy that any thousand of the really wicked Tartuffes could have committed. He grows and grows. His scraps of learning, as long as those more ignorant than himself are his audience; his mock humility anxious for praise; his parade of generous and sententious sentiment; his pretence—pretence—pretence—all arising from no evil machinations whatever, but from a morbid and restless craving for esteem. Hence, horrible shadow! Let us put out the candles and get to bed.

But next morning, as we find ourselves out on the blue Atlantic again, with Ru-na-Gaul lighthouse left far behind, and the pale line of Coll at the horizon, we begin to see why the skill and patient assiduity of this amateur psychologist should have raised that ghost for us the night before. Her uncle is coming. He is not one of the plausible kind. And if it should be necessary to invite him on board, might we not the more readily tolerate his cynical bluntness and rudeness, after we have been taught to abhor as the hatefullest of mortals the well-meaning hypocrite whose vanity makes his life a bundle of small lies? Very clever indeed, Miss Avon—very clever. But don't you raise any more ghosts; they are unpleasant company—even as an antidote. And now, John of Skye, if it must be that we are to encounter this pestilent creature at the end of our voyage, clap on all sail now, and take us right royally down through these far islands of the west. Ah! do we not know them of old? Soon as we get round the Cailleach Point we descry the nearest of them amid the loneliness of the wide Atlantic sea. For there is Carnaburg, with her spur of rock; and Fladda, long and rugged, and bare; and Lunga, with her peak; and the Dutchman's Cap—a pale blue in the south. How bravely the *White Dove* swings on her way—springing like a bird over the western swell! And as we get past Ru-Treshnish, behold! another group of islands—Gometra and the green-shored Ulva, that guard the entrance to Loch Tua; and Colonsay, the haunt of the sea birds; and the rock of Erisgeir—all shining in the sun. And then we hear a strange sound—different from the light rush of the waves—a low, and sullen, and distant booming, such as one faintly hears in a sea-shell. As the *White Dove* ploughs on her way, we come nearer and nearer to this wonder of the deep—the ribbed and fantastic shores of Staffa; and we see how the great Atlantic rollers, making for the cliffs of Gribun and Burg, are caught by those outer rocks and torn into masses of white foam, and sent roaring and thundering into the blackness of the caves. We pass close by; the air trembles with the shock of that mighty surge; there is a mist of spray rising into the summer air. And then we sail away again; and the day wears on as the white-winged *White Dove* bounds over the heavy seas; and Mary Avon—as we draw near the Ross of Mull, all glowing in the golden evening—is singing a song of Ulva.

But there is no time for romance, as the *White Dove* (drawing eight feet of water) makes in for the shallow harbour outside Bunessan.

"Down foresail!" calls out our John of Skye; and by and by her head comes up to the wind, the great mainsail flapping in the breeze. And again, "Down chub, boys!" and there is another rattle and roar amid the silence of this solitary little bay. The herons croak their fright and fly away on heavy wing; the curlews whistle shrilly; the sea-pyots whirr along the lonely shores. And then our good Friedrich d'or sounds his silver-toned bell.

The stillness of this summer evening on deck; the glory deepening over the wide Atlantic; the delightful laughter of the Laird over those "good ones" about Homesh; the sympathetic glance of Mary Avon's soft black eyes: did we not value them all the more that we knew we had something far different to look forward to? Even as we idled away the beautiful and lambent night, we had a vague consciousness that our enemy was stealthily drawing near. In a day or two at the most we should find the grim spectre of the East Wind in the rose-garden of Castle Osprey.

CHAPTER V.
A BRAVE CAREER.

But when we went on deck the next morning we forgot all about the detestable person who was about to break in upon our peace (there was small chance that our faithful Angus Sutherland might encounter the snake in this summer paradise, and trample on him, and pitch him out; for this easy way of getting rid of disagreeable folk is not permitted in the Highlands nowadays) as we looked on the beautiful bay shining all around us.

"Dear me!" said Denny-mains, "if Tom Galbraith could only see that now! It is a great peety he has never been to this place. I'm thinking I must write to him."

The Laird did not remember that we had an artist on board—one who, if she was not so great an artist as Mr. Galbraith, had at least exhibited one or two small landscapes in oil at the Royal Academy. But then the Academicians, though they might dread the contrast between their own work and that of Tom Galbraith, could have no fear of Mary Avon.

And even Mr. Galbraith himself might have been puzzled to find among his pigments any equivalent for the rare and clear colours of this morning scene as now we sailed away from Bunessan with a light topsail breeze. How blue the day was—blue skies, blue seas, a faint transparent blue along the cliffs of Burg and Gribun, a darker blue where the far Ru-Treshanish ran out into the sea, a shadow of blue to mark where the caves of Staffa retreated from the surface of the sun-brown rocks! And here, nearer at hand, the warmer colours of the shore—the soft, velvety olive-greens of the moss and breckan; the splashes of lilac where the rocks were bare of herbage; the tender sunny reds where the granite promontories ran out to the sea; the beautiful cream-whites of the sandy bays!

Here, too, are the islands again as we get out into the open—Gometra, with its one white house at the point; and Inch Kenneth, where the seals show their shining black heads among the shallows; and Erisgeir and Colonsay, where the skarts alight to dry their wings on the rocks; and Staffa, and Lunga, and the Dutchman, lying peaceful enough now on the calm blue seas. We have time to look at them, for the wind is slight, and the broad-beamed *White Dove* is not a quick sailer in a light breeze. The best part of the forenoon is over before we find ourselves opposite to the gleaming white sands of the northern bays of Iona.

"But surely both of us together will be able to make him stay longer than ten days," says the elder of the two women to the younger—and you may be sure she was not speaking of East Wind.

Mary Avon looks up with a start; then looks down again—perhaps with the least touch of colour in her face—as she says hurriedly—

"Oh, I think you will. He is your friend. As for me—you see—I—I scarcely know him."

"Oh, Mary!" says the other reproachfully. "You have been meeting him constantly all these two months; you must know him better than any of us. I am sure I wish he was on board now—he could tell us all about the geology of the islands, and what not. It will be delightful to have somebody on board who knows something."

Such is the gratitude of women!—and the Laird had just been describing to her some further points of the famous heresy case.

"And then he knows Gaelic!" says the elder woman. "He will tell us what all the names of the islands mean."

"Oh, yes," says the younger one, "he understands Gaelic very well, though he cannot speak much of it."

"And I think he is very fond of boats," remarks our hostess.

"Oh, exceedingly—exceedingly!" says the other, who, if she does not know Angus Sutherland, seems to have picked up some information about him somehow. "You cannot imagine how he has been looking forward to sailing with you; he has scarcely had any holiday for years."

"Then he must stay longer than ten days," says the elder woman; adding with a smile, "you know, Mary, it is not the number of his patients that will hurry him back to London."

"Oh, but I assure you," says Miss Avon seriously, "that he is not at all anxious to have many patients—as yet! Oh, no!—I never knew any one who was so indifferent about money. I know he would live on bread and water—if that were necessary—to go on with his researches. He told me himself that all the time he was at Leipsic his expenses were never more than 1*l.* a week."

She seemed to know a good deal about the circumstances of this young F.R.S.

"Look at what he has done with those anæsthetics," continues Miss Avon. "Isn't it better to find out something that does good to the whole world than give yourself up to making money by wheedling a lot of old women?"

This estimate of the physician's art was not flattering.

"But," she says warmly, "if the Government had any sense, that is just the sort of man they would put in a position to go on with his invaluable work. And Oxford and Cambridge, with all their wealth, they scarcely even recognise the noblest profession that a man can devote himself to—when even the poor Scotch Universities and the Universities all over Europe have always had their medical and scientific chairs. I think it is perfectly disgraceful!"

Since when had she become so strenuous an advocate of the endowment of research?

"Why, look at Dr. Sutherland—when he is burning to get on with his own proper work—when his name is beginning to be known all over Europe—he has to fritter away his time in editing a scientific magazine and in those hospital lectures. And that, I suppose, is barely enough to live on. But I know," she says, with decision, "that in spite of everything—I know that before he is five-and-thirty, he will be President of the British Association."

Here, indeed, is a brave career for the Scotch student: cannot one complete the sketch as it roughly exists in the minds of those two women?

At twenty-one, B.M. of Edinburgh.

At twenty-six, F.R.S.

At thirty, Professor of Biology at Oxford: the chair founded through the intercession of the women of Great Britain.

At thirty-five, President of the British Association.

At forty, a baronetcy, for further discoveries in the region of anæsthetics.

At forty-five, consulting physician to half the gouty old gentlemen of England, and amassing an immense fortune.

At fifty——

Well, at fifty, is it not time that "the poor Scotch student," now become great and famous and wealthy, should look around for some beautiful princess to share his high estate with him? He has not had time before to think of such matters. But what is this now? Is it that microscopes and test-tubes have dimmed his eyes? Is it that honours and responsibilities have silvered his hair? Or, is the drinking deep of the Pactolus stream a deadly poison? There is no beautiful princess awaiting him anywhere. He is alone among his honours. There was once a beautiful princess—beautiful-souled and tender-eyed, if not otherwise too lovely—awaiting him among the Western Seas; but that time is over and gone many a year ago. The opportunity has passed. Ambition called him away, and he left her; and the last he saw of her was when he bade good-bye to the *White Dove*.

What have we to do with these idle dreams? We are getting within sight of Iona village now; and the sun is shining on the green shores, and on the ruins of the old cathedral, and on that white house just above the cornfield. And as there is no good anchorage about the island, we have to make in for a little creek on the Mull side of the Sound, called Polterriv, or the Bull-hole; and this creek is narrow, tortuous, and shallow; and a yacht drawing eight feet of water has to be guided with some circumspection—especially if you go up to the inner harbour above the rock called the Little Bull. And so we make inquiries of John of Skye, who has not been with us here before. It is even hinted, that if he is not quite sure of the channel, we might send the gig over to Iona for John Macdonald, who is an excellent pilot.

"John Macdonald!" exclaims John of Skye, whose professional pride has been wounded. "Will John Macdonald be doing anything more than I wass do myself in the Bull-hole—ay, last year—last year I will tek my own smack out of the Bull-hole at the norse end, and ferry near low water, too; and her deep-loaded? Oh, yes, I will be knowing the Bull-hole this many a year."

And John of Skye is as good as his word. Favoured by a flood-tide, we steal gently into the unfrequented creek, behind the great rocks of red granite; and so extraordinarily clear is the water that, standing upright on the deck, we can see the white sand of the bottom with shoals of young saithe darting this way and that. And then just as we get opposite an opening in the rocks, through which we can descry the northern shores of Iona, and above those the blue peak of the Dutchman, away goes the anchor with a short, quick rush; her head swings round to meet the tide; the *White Dove* is safe from all the winds that blow. Now lower away the gig, boys, and bear us over the blue waters of the Sound!

"I am really afraid to begin," Mary Avon says, as we remonstrate with her for not having touched a colour-tube since she started. "Besides, you know, I scarcely look on it that we have really set out yet. This is only a sort of shaking ourselves into our places; I am only getting accustomed to the ways of our cabin now. I shall scarcely consider that we have started on our real voyaging until———"

Oh, yes, we know very well. Until we have got Angus Sutherland on board. But what she really said was, after slight hesitation:

"———until we set out for the Northern Hebrides."

"Ay, it's a good thing to feel nervous about beginning," says the Laird, as the long sweep of the four oars brings us nearer and nearer to the Iona shores. "I have often heard Tom Galbraith say that to the younger men. He says if a young man is over confident, he'll come to nothing. But there was a good one I once heard Galbraith tell about a young man that was pentin at Tarbert—that's Tarbert on Loch Fyne, Miss Avon. Ay, well, he was pentin away, and he was putting in the young lass of the house as a fisher-lass; and he asked her if she could not get a creel to strap on her back, as a background for her head, ye know. Well, says she———"

Here the fierce humour of the story began to bubble up in the Laird's blue-grey eyes. We were all half laughing already. It was impossible to resist the glow of delight on the Laird's face.

"Says she—just as pat as ninepence—says she, 'it's your ain head that wants a creel!'"

The explosion was inevitable. The roar of laughter at this good one was so infectious that a subdued smile played over the rugged features of John of Skye. "*It's your ain head that wants a creel!*" the Laird laughed, and laughed again, until the last desperately suppressed sounds were something like *kee! kee! kee!* Even Mary Avon pretended to understand.

"There was a real good one," says he, obviously overjoyed to have so appreciative an audience, "that I mind of reading in the Dean's *Reminiscences*. It was about an old leddy in Edinburgh who met in a shop a young officer she had seen before. He was a tall young man, and she eyed him from head to heel, and says she—ha! ha!—says she, '*Od, ye're a lang lad: God gie ye grace.*' Dry—very dry—wasn't it? There was real humour in that—a pawky humour that people in the South cannot understand at all. '*Od*, says she, '*ye're a lang lad: God grant ye grace.*' There was a great dale of character in that."

We were sure of it; but still we preferred the Laird's stories about Homesh. We invariably liked best the stories at which the Laird laughed most—whether we quite understood their pawky humour or not.

"Dr. Sutherland has a great many stories about the Highlanders," says Miss Avon timidly; "they are very amusing."

"As far as I have observed," remarked the Laird—for how could he relish the notion of having a rival anecdote-monger on board?—"as far as I have observed, the Highland character is entirely without humour. Ay, I have heard Tom Galbraith say that very often, and he has been everywhere in the Highlands."

"Well, then," says Mary Avon, with a quick warmth of indignation in her face—how rapidly those soft dark eyes could change their expression!—"I hope Mr. Galbraith knows more about painting than he knows about the Highlanders! I thought that anybody who knows anything knows that the Celtic nature is full of imagination, and humour, and pathos, and poetry; and the Saxon—the Saxon!—it is his business to plod over ploughed fields, and be as dull and commonplace as the other animals he sees there!"

Gracious goodness!—here was a tempest! The Laird was speechless; for, indeed, at this moment we bumped against the sacred shores—that is to say, the landing-slip—of Iona; and had to scramble on to the big stones. Then we walked up and past the cottages, and through the potato-field, and past the white inn, and so to the hallowed shrine and its graves of the kings. We spent the whole of the afternoon there.

When we got back to the yacht and to dinner we discovered that a friend had visited us in our absence, and had left of his largesse behind him—nasturtiums and yellow-and-white pansies, and what not—to say nothing of fresh milk, and crisp, delightful lettuce. We drank his health.

Was it the fear of some one breaking in on our domestic peace that made that last evening among the western islands so lovely to us? We went out in the gig after dinner; the Laird put forth his engines of destruction to encompass the innocent lythe; we heard him humming the "Haughs o' Cromdale" in the silence. The wonderful glory of that evening!—Iona become an intense olive-green against the gold and crimson of the sunset; the warm light shining along the red granite of western Mull. Then the yellow moon rose in the south—into the calm violet-hued vault of the heavens; and there was a golden fire on the ripples and on the wet blades of the oars as we rowed back with laughter and singing.

Sing tantara! sing tantara!
Sing tantara! sing tantara!
Said he, the Highland army rues
That ere they came to Cromdale!

And then, next morning, we were up at five o'clock. If we were going to have a tooth pulled, why not have the little interview over at once? East Wind would be waiting for us at Castle Osprey.

Blow, soft westerly breeze, then, and bear us down by Fion-phort, and round the granite Ross—shining all a pale red in the early dawn. And here is Ardalanish Point; and there, as the morning goes by, are the Carsaig arches, and then Loch Buy, and finally the blue Firth of Lorn. Northward now, and still northward—until, far away, the white house shining amidst the firs, and the flag fluttering in the summer air. Have they descried us, then? Or is the bunting hoisted in honour of guests? The pale cheek of Mary Avon tells a tale as she descries that far signal; but that is no business of ours. Perhaps it is only of her uncle that she is thinking.

CHAPTER VI.
OUR NEW GUESTS.

Behold, now!—this beautiful garden of Castle Osprey all ablaze in the sun—the roses, pansies, poppies, and what not bewildering our eyes after the long looking at the blue water and, in the midst of the brilliant paradise—just as we had feared—the snake! He did not scurry away at our approach, as snakes are wont to do; or raise his horrent head, and hiss. The fact is, we found him comfortably seated under a drooping ash, smoking. He rose and explained that he had strolled up from the shore to await our coming. He did not seem to notice that Mary Avon, as she came along, had to walk slowly, and was leaning on the arm of the Laird.

Certainly nature had not been bountiful to this short, spare person who had now come among us. He had closely-cropped, coarse grey hair; an eagle beak; a certain pink and raw appearance of the face, as if perpetual east winds had chafed the skin; and a most pernicious habit of loudly clearing his husky throat. Then with the aggressive nose went a well-defined pugilist's jaw and a general hang-dog scowl about the mouth. For the rest Mr. Smethurst seemed desirous of making up for those unpleasant features which nature had bestowed upon him by a studied air of self-possession, and by an extreme precision of dress. Alack, and well-a-day! these laudable efforts were of little avail. Nature was too strong for him. The assumption of a languid air was not quite in consonance with the ferrety grey eyes and the bull-dog mouth; the precision of his costume only gave him the look of a well-dressed groom, or a butler gone on the turf. There was not much grateful to the sight about Mr. Frederick Smethurst.

But were we to hate the man for being ugly? Despite his raw face, he might have the white soul of an angel. And in fact we knew absolutely nothing against his public character or private reputation, except that he had once gone through the Bankruptcy Court; and even of that little circumstance our womenfolk were not aware. However, there was no doubt at all that a certain coldness—apparent to us who knew her well—marked the manner of this small lady who now went up and shook hands with him, and declared—unblushingly—that she was so glad he had run up to the Highlands.

"And you know," said she, with that charming politeness which she would show to the arch-fiend himself if he were properly introduced to her, "you know, Mr. Smethurst, that yachting is such an uncertain thing, one never knows when one may get back; but if you could spare a few days to take a run with us, you would see what a capital mariner Mary has become, and I am sure it would be a great pleasure to us."

These were actually her words. She uttered them without the least tremor of hesitation. She looked him straight in the face with those clear, innocent, confiding eyes of hers. How could the man tell that she was wishing him at Jericho?

And it was in silence that we waited to hear our doom pronounced. A yachting trip with this intolerable Jonah on board! The sunlight went out of the day; the blue went out of the sky and the seas; the world was filled with gloom, and chaos, and East Wind!

Imagine, then, the sudden joy with which we heard of our deliverance! Surely it was not the raucous voice of Frederick Smethurst, but a sound of summer bells.

"Oh, thank you," he said, in his affectedly indifferent way; "but the fact is, I have run up to see Mary only on a little matter of business, and I must get back at once. Indeed, I purpose leaving by the Dalmally coach in the afternoon. Thank you very much, though; perhaps some other time I may be more fortunate."

How we had wronged this poor man! We hated him no longer. On the contrary, great grief was expressed over his departure; and he was begged at least to stay that one evening. No doubt he had heard of Dr. Angus Sutherland, who had made such discoveries in the use of anæsthetics? Dr. Sutherland was coming by the afternoon steamer. Would not he stay and meet him at dinner?

Our tears broke out afresh—metaphorically—when East Wind persisted in his intention of departure; but of course compulsion was out of the question. And so we allowed him to go into the house, to have that business interview with his niece.

"A poor crayture!" remarked the Laird confidently, forgetting that he was talking of a friend of ours. "Why does he not speak out like a man, instead of drawling and dawdling? His accent is jist insufferable."

"And what business can he have with Mary?" says our sovereign lady sharply—just as if a man with a raw skin and an eagle-beak must necessarily be a pickpocket. "He was the trustee of that little fortune of hers, I know; but that is all over. She got the money when she came of age. What can he want to see her about now?"

We concerned ourselves not with that. It was enough for us that the snake was about to retreat from our summer paradise of his own free will and pleasure. And Angus

Sutherland was coming; and the provisioning of the yacht had to be seen to; for tomorrow—to-morrow we spread our white wings again and take flight to the far north!

Never was parting guest so warmly speeded. We concealed our tears as the coach rolled away. We waved a hand to him. And then, when it was suggested that the wagonette that had brought Mary Avon down from Castle Osprey might just as well go along to the quay—for the steamer bringing Dr. Sutherland would be in shortly—and when we actually did set out in that direction, there was so little grief on our faces that you could not have told we had been bidding farewell to a valued friend and relative.

Now if our good-hearted Laird had had a grain of jealousy in his nature, he might well have resented the manner in which these two women spoke of the approaching guest. In their talk the word "he" meant only one person. "He" was sure to come by this steamer. "He" was so punctual in his engagements. Would he bring a gun or a rod; or would the sailing be enough amusement for him? What a capital thing it was for him to be able to take an interest in some such out-of-door exercise, as a distraction to the mind! And so forth, and so forth. The Laird heard all this, and his expectations were no doubt rising and rising. Forgetful of his disappointment on first seeing Mary Avon, he was in all likelihood creating an imaginary figure of Angus Sutherland—and, of course, this marvel of erudition and intellectual power must be a tall, wan, pale person, with the travail of thinking written in lines across the spacious brow. The Laird was not aware that for many a day after we first made the acquaintance of the young Scotch student he was generally referred to in our private conversation as "Brose."

And, indeed, the Laird did stare considerably when he saw—elbowing his way through the crowd and making for us with a laugh of welcome on the fresh-coloured face— a stout-set, muscular, blue-eyed, sandy-haired, good-humoured-looking, youngish man; who, instead of having anything Celtic about his appearance, might have been taken for the son of a south-country farmer. Our young Doctor was carrying his own portmanteau, and sturdily shoving his way through the porters who would fain have seized it.

"I am glad to see you, Angus," said our queen regent, holding out her hand; and there was no ceremonial politeness in that reception—but you should have seen the look in her eyes.

Then he went on to the waggonette.

"How do you do, Miss Avon?" said he, quite timidly, like a school-boy. He scarcely glanced up at her face, which was regarding him with a very pleasant welcome; he seemed relieved when he had to turn and seize his portmanteau again. Knowing that he was rather fond of driving, our mistress and admiral-in-chief offered him the reins, but he declined the honour; Mary Avon was sitting in front. "Oh, no, thank you," said he quite hastily, and with something uncommonly like a blush. The Laird, if he had been entertaining any feeling of jealousy, must have been reassured. This Doctor-fellow was no formidable rival. He spoke very little—he only listened—as we drove away to Castle Osprey. Mary Avon was chatting briskly and cheerfully, and it was to the Laird that she addressed that running fire of nonsense and merry laughter.

But the young Doctor was greatly concerned when, on our arrival at Castle Osprey, he saw Mary Avon helped down with much care, and heard the story of the sprain.

"Who bandages your ankle?" said he at once, and without any shyness now.

"I do it myself," said she cheerfully. "I can do it well enough."

"Oh, no, you cannot!" said he abruptly; "a person stooping cannot. The bandage should be as tight, and as smooth, as the skin of a drum. You must let some one else do that for you."

And he was disposed to resent this walking about in the garden before dinner. What business had she to trifle with such a serious matter as a sprain? And a sprain which was the recall of an older sprain. "Did she wish to be lame for life?" he asked sharply.

Mary Avon laughed, and said that worse things than that had befallen people. He asked her whether she found any pleasure in voluntary martyrdom; she blushed a little, and turned to the Laird.

The Laird was at this moment laying before us the details of a most gigantic scheme. It appeared that the inhabitants of Strathgovan, not content with a steam fire-engine, were talking about having a public park—actually proposing to have a public park, with beds of flowers, and iron seats; and, to crown all, a gymnasium, where the youths of the neighbourhood might twirl themselves on the gay trapeze to their hearts' content. And where the subscriptions were to come from; and what were the hardiest plants for borders; and whether the gymnasium should be furnished with ropes or with chains—these matters were weighing heavily on the mind of our good friend of Denny-mains. Angus Sutherland relapsed into silence, and gazed absently at a tree-fuchsia that stood by.

"It is a beautiful tree, is it not?" said a voice beside him—that of our midge-like empress.

He started.

"Oh, yes," he said cheerfully. "I was thinking I should like to live the life of a tree like that, dying in the winter, you know, and being quite impervious to frost, and snow, and hard weather; and then, as soon as the fine warm spring and summer came round, coming to life again and spreading yourself out to feel all the sunlight and the warm winds. That must be a capital life."

"But do you really think they can feel that? Why, you must believe that those trees and flowers are alive!"

"Does anybody doubt it?" said he quite simply. "They are certainly alive. Why——"

And here he bethought himself for a moment.

"If I only had a good microscope now," said he eagerly, "I would show you the life of a plant directly—in every cell of it: did you never see the constant life in each cell—the motion of the chlorophyll granules circling and circling night and day? Did no one ever show you that?"

Well, no one had ever shown us that. We may now and again have entertained angels unawares; but we were not always stumbling against Fellows of the Royal Society.

"Then I must borrow one somewhere," said he decisively, "and show you the secret life of even the humblest plant that exists. And then look what a long life it is, in the case of the perennial plants. Did you ever think of that? Those great trees in the Yosemite valley—they were alive and feeling the warm sunlight and the winds about them when Alfred was hiding in the marshes; and they were living the same undisturbed life when Charles the First had his head chopped off; and they were living—in peace and quietness—when all Europe had to wake up to stamp out the Napoleonic pest; and they are alive now and quite careless of the little creatures that come to span out their circumference, and ticket them, and give them ridiculous names. Had any of the patriarchs a life as long as that?"

The Laird eyed this young man askance. There was something uncanny about him. What might not he say when—in the northern solitudes to which we were going—the great Semple heresy-case was brought on for discussion?

But at dinner the Laird got on very well with our new guest; for the latter listened most respectfully when Denny-mains was demonstrating the exceeding purity, and strength, and fitness of the speech used in the south of Scotland. And indeed the Laird was generous. He admitted that there were blemishes. He deprecated the introduction of French words; and gave us a much longer list of those aliens than usually appears in books. What about *conjee*, and *que-vee*, and *fracaw* as used by Scotch children and old wives?

Then after dinner—at nine o'clock the wonderful glow of the summer evening was still filling the drawing-room—the Laird must needs have Mary Avon sing to him. It was not a custom of hers. She rarely would sing a song of set purpose. The linnet sings all day—when you do not watch her; but she will not sing if you go and ask.

However, on this occasion, her hostess went to the piano, and sat down to play the accompaniment; and Mary Avon stood beside her and sang, in rather a low voice—but it was tender enough—some modern version of the old ballad of the Queen's Maries. What were the words? These were of them, any way:—

Yestreen the Queen had four Maries;
This night she'll hae but three:
There was Mary Beaton, and Mary Seaton,
And Mary Carmichael, and me.

19

But indeed, if you had seen that graceful slim figure—clad all in black velvet, with the broad band of gold fringe round the neck—and the small, shapely, smoothly-brushed head above the soft swathes of white muslin—and if you had caught a glimpse of the black eyelashes drooping outward from the curve of the pale cheek—and if you had heard the tender, low voice of Mary Avon, you might have forgotten about the Queen's Maries altogether.

And then Dr. Sutherland: the Laird was determined—in true Scotch fashion—that everybody who could not sing should be goaded to sing.

"Oh, well," said the young man, with a laugh, "you know a student in Germany must sing whether he can or not. And I learned there to smash out something like an accompaniment also."

And he went to the piano without more ado and did smash out an accompaniment. And if his voice was rather harsh?—well, we should have called it raucous in the case of East Wind, but we only called it manly and strenuous when it was Angus Sutherland who sang. And it was a manly song, too—a fitting song for our last night on shore, the words hailing from the green woods of Fuinary, the air an air that had many a time been heard among the western seas. It was the song of the Biorlinn[#] that he sang to us; we could hear the brave chorus and the splash of the long oars:—

Send the biorlinn on careering!
Cheerily and all together—
Ho, ro, clansmen!
A long, strong pull together—
Ho, ro, clansmen!

Give her way and show her wake
'Mid showering spray and curling eddies—
Ho, ro, clansmen!
A long, strong pull together—
Ho, ro, clansmen!

Do we not hear now the measured stroke in the darkness of the morning? The water springs from her bows; one by one the headlands are passed. But lo! the day is breaking; the dawn will surely bring a breeze with it; and then the sail of the gallant craft will bear her over the seas:—

Another cheer, our Isle appears!
Our biorlinn bears her on the faster—
Ho, ro, clansmen!
A long, strong pull together—
Ho, ro, clansmen!

Ahead she goes! the land she knows!
Behold! the snowy shores of Canna—
Ho, ro, clansmen!
A long, strong pull together—
Ho, ro, clansmen!

A long, strong pull together indeed: who could resist joining in the thunder of the chorus? And we were bound for Canna, too: this was our last night on shore.

[#] *Biorlinn*—that is, a rowing-boat. The word is pronounced *byurlen*. The song, which in a measure imitates the rhythm peculiar to Highland poetry—consisting in a certain repetition of the same vowel sounds—is the production of Dr. Macleod, of Morven. And here, for the benefit of any one who minds such things, is a rough draft of the air, arranged by a most charming young lady, who, however, says she would much rather die than have her name mentioned:—

Music fragments

Our last night on shore. In such circumstances one naturally has a glance round at the people with whom one is to be brought into such close contact for many and many a day.

But in this particular case, what was the use of speculating, or grumbling, or remonstrating? There is a certain household that is ruled with a rod of iron. And if the mistress of that household chose to select as her summer companions a "shilpit bit thing," and a hard-headed, ambitious Scotch student, and a parochial magnate haunted by a heresy-case, how dared one object? There is such a thing as peace and quietness.

But however unpromising the outlook might be, do we not know the remark that is usually made by that hard-worked officer, the chief mate, when, on the eve of a voyage, he finds himself confronted by an unusually mongrel crew? He regards those loafers and outcasts—from the Bowery, and Ratcliffe Highway, and the Broomielaw—Greeks, niggers, and Mexicans—with a critical and perhaps scornful air, and forthwith proceeds to address them in the following highly polished manner:—

"By etcetera-etcetera, you are an etceteraed rum-looking lot; but etcetera-etcetera me *if I don't lick you into shape before we get to Rio.*"

And so—good-night!—and let all good people pray for fair skies and a favouring breeze! And if there is any song to be heard in our dreams, let it be the song of the Queen's Maries—in the low, tender voice of Mary Avon:—

There was Mary Beaton, and Mary Seaton,
And Mary Carmichael, and me.

CHAPTER VII.
NORTHWARD.

We have bidden good-bye to the land; the woods and the green hills have become pale in the haze of the summer light; we are out here, alone, on the shining blue plain. And if our young Doctor betrays a tendency to keep forward—conversing with John of Skye about blocks, and tackle, and winches; and if the Laird—whose parental care and regard for Mary Avon is becoming beautiful to see—should have quite a monopoly of the young lady, and be more bent than ever on amusing her with his "good ones;" and if our queen and governor should spend a large portion of her time below, in decorating cabins with flowers, in overhauling napery, and in earnest consultation with Master Fred about certain culinary mysteries; notwithstanding all these divergences of place and occupation, our little kingdom afloat is compact enough. There is always, for example, a reassembling at meals. There is an instant community of interest when a sudden cry calls all hands on deck to regard some new thing—the spouting of a whale or the silvery splashing of a shoal of mackerel. But now—but now—if only some cloud-compelling Jove would break this insufferably fine weather, and give us a tearing good gale!

It is a strange little kingdom. It has no postal service. Shilling telegrams are unknown in it; there is no newspaper at breakfast. There are no barrel-organs; nor rattling hansoms raising the dust in windy streets; there is no afternoon scandal; overheated rooms at midnight are a thing of the past. Serene, independent, self-centred, it minds its own affairs; if the whole of Europe were roaring for war, not even an echo of the cry would reach us. We only hear the soft calling of the sea-birds as we sit and read, or talk, or smoke; from time to time watching the shadows move on the blistering hot decks, or guessing at the names of the blue mountains that rise above Loch Etive and Lochaber. At the present moment there is a faint summer haze over these mountains; as yet we have around us none of the dazzling light and strangely intense colours that are peculiar to this part of the world, and that are only possible, in fact, in an atmosphere frequently washed clear by squalls of rain. This question of rain turns up at lunch.

"They prayed for rain in the churches last Sunday—so Captain John says," Mary Avon remarks.

"The distilleries are stopped: that's very serious," continues the Laird.

"Well," says Queen T., "people talk about the rain in the West Highlands. It must be true, as everybody says it is true. But now—excepting the year we went to America with Sylvia Balfour—we have been here for five years running; and each year we made up our mind for a deluge—thinking we had deserved it, you know. Well, it never came. Look at this now."

And the fact was that we were lying motionless on the smooth bosom of the Atlantic, with the sun so hot on the decks that we were glad to get below.

"Very strange—very strange, indeed," remarked the Laird, with a profound air. "Now what value are we to put on any historical evidence if we find such a conflict of testimony about what is at our own doors? How should there be two opeenions about the weather in the West Highlands? It is a matter of common experience—dear me! I never heard the like."

"Oh, but I think we might try to reconcile those diverse opinions!" said Angus Sutherland, with an absolute gravity. "You hear mostly the complaints of London people, who make much of a passing shower. Then the tourist and holiday folk, especially from the South, come in the autumn, when the fine summer weather has broken. And then," he added, addressing himself with a frank smile to the small creature who had been expressing her wonder over the fine weather, "perhaps, if you are pleased with your holiday on the whole, you are not anxious to remember the wet days; and then you are not afraid of a shower, I know; and besides that, when one is yachting, one is more anxious for wind than for fine weather."

"Oh, I am sure that is it!" called out Mary Avon quite eagerly. She did not care how she destroyed the Laird's convictions about the value of historical evidence. "That is an explanation of the whole thing."

At this, our young Doctor—who had been professing to treat this matter seriously merely as a joke—quickly lowered his eyes. He scarcely ever looked Mary Avon in the face when she spoke to him, or when he had to speak to her. And a little bit of shy embarrassment in his manner towards her—perceivable only at times—was all the more singular in a man who was shrewd and hard-headed enough, who had knocked about the world and seen many persons and things, and who had a fair amount of unassuming self-confidence, mingled with a vein of sly and reticent humour. He talked freely enough when he was addressing our admiral-in-chief. He was not afraid to meet *her* eyes. Indeed, they were so familiar friends that she called him by his Christian name—a practice which in general she detested. But she would as soon have thought of applying "Mr." to one of her own boys at Epsom College as to Angus Sutherland.

"Well, you know, Angus," says she pleasantly, "you have definitely promised to go up to the Outer Hebrides with us, and back. The longer the calms last, the longer we shall have you. So we shall gladly put up with the fine weather."

"It is very kind of you to say so; but I have already had such a long holiday——"

"Oh!" said Mary Avon, with her eyes full of wonder and indignation. She was too surprised to say any more. She only stared at him. She knew he had been working night and day in Edinburgh.

"I mean," said he hastily, and looking down, "I have been away so long from London. Indeed, I was getting rather anxious about my next month's number; but luckily, just before I left Edinburgh, a kind friend sent me a most valuable paper, so I am quite at ease again. Would you like to read it, sir? It is set up in type."

He took the sheets from his pocket, and handed them to the Laird. Denny-mains looked at the title. It was *On the Radiolarians of the Coal Measures*, and it was the production of a well-known professor. The Laird handed back the paper without opening it.

"No, thank you," said he, with some dignity. "If I wished to be instructed, I would like a safer guide than that man."

We looked with dismay on this dangerous thing that had been brought on board: might it not explode and blow up the ship?

"Why," said our Doctor, in unaffected wonder, and entirely mistaking the Laird's exclamation, "he is a perfect master of his subject."

"There is a great deal too much speculation nowadays on these matters, and parteecularly among the younger men," remarked the Laird severely. And he looked at Angus Sutherland. "I suppose now ye are well acquainted with the *Vestiges of Creation*?"

"I have heard of the book," said Brose—regretfully confessing his ignorance—"but I never happened to see it."

The Laird's countenance lightened.

"So much the better—so much the better. A most mischievous and unsettling book. But all the harm it can do is counteracted by a noble work—a conclusive work that leaves nothing to be said. Ye have read the *Testimony of the Rocks*, no doubt?"

"Oh, yes, certainly," our Doctor was glad to be able to say; "but—but it was a long time ago—when I was a boy, in fact."

"Boy, or man, you'll get no better book on the history of the earth. I tell ye, sir, I never read a book that placed such firm conviction in my mind. Will ye get any of the new men they are talking about as keen an observer and as skilful in arguing as Hugh Miller? No, no; not one of them dares to try to upset the *Testimony of the Rocks*."

Angus Sutherland appealed against this sentence of finality only in a very humble way.

"Of course, sir," said he meekly, "you know that science is still moving forward——"

"Science?" repeated the Laird. "Science may be moving forward or moving backward; but can it upset the facts of the earth? Science may say what it likes; but the facts remain the same."

Now this point was so conclusive that we unanimously hailed the Laird as victor. Our young Doctor submitted with an excellent good humour. He even promised to post that paper on the Radiolarians at the very first post-office we might reach: we did not want any such explosive compounds on board.

That night we only got as far as Fishnish Bay—a solitary little harbour probably down on but few maps; and that we had to reach by getting out the gig for a tow. There was a strange bronze-red in the northern skies, long after the sun had set; but in here the shadow of the great mountains was on the water. We could scarcely see the gig; but Angus Sutherland had joined the men and was pulling stroke; and along with the measured splash of the oars, we heard something about "*Ho, ro, clansmen!*" Then, in the cool night air, there was a slight fragrance of peat-smoke; we knew we were getting near the shore.

"He's a fine fellow, that," says the Laird, generously, of his defeated antagonist. "A fine fellow. His knowledge of different things is just remarkable; and he's as modest as a girl. Ay, and he can row, too; a while ago when it was lighter, I could see him put his shoulders into it. Ay, he's a fine, good-natured fellow, and I am glad he has not been led astray by that mischievous book, the *Vestiges of Creation*."

Come on board now, boys, and swing up the gig to the davits! Twelve fathoms of chain?—away with her then!—and there is a roar in the silence of the lonely little bay. And thereafter silence; and the sweet fragrance of the peat in the night air, and the appearance, above the black hills, of a clear, shining, golden planet that sends a quivering line of light across the water to us. And, once more, good-night and pleasant dreams!

But what is this in the morning? There have been no pleasant dreams for John of Skye and his merry men during the last night; for here we are already between Mingary Bay and Ru-na-Gaul Lighthouse; and before us is the open Atlantic, blue under the fair skies of the morning. And here is Dr. Sutherland, at the tiller, with a suspiciously negligent look about his hair and shirt-collar.

"I have been up since four," says he, with a laugh. "I heard them getting under way, and did not wish to miss anything. You know these places are not so familiar to me as they are to you."

"Is there going to be any wind to-day, John?"

"No mich," says John of Skye, looking at the cloudless blue vault above the glassy sweeps of the sea.

Nevertheless, as the morning goes by, we get as much of a breeze as enables us to draw away from the mainland—round Ardnamurchan ("the headland of the great sea") and out into the open—with Muick Island, and the sharp Scuir of Eigg, and the peaks of Rum lying over there on the still Atlantic, and far away in the north the vast and spectral mountains of Skye.

And now the work of the day begins. Mary Avon, for mere shame's sake, is at last compelled to produce one of her blank canvases and open her box of tubes. And now it would appear that Angus Sutherland—though deprived of the authority of the sick-room— is beginning to lose his fear of the English young lady. He makes himself useful—not with the elaborate and patronising courtesy of the Laird, but in a sort of submissive, matter-of-fact shifty fashion. He sheathes the spikes of her easel with cork so that they shall not mark the deck. He rigs up, to counterbalance that lack of stability, a piece of cord with a heavy weight. Then, with the easel fixed, he fetches her a deck-chair to sit in, and a deck-stool for her colours, and these and her he places under the lee of the foresail, to be out of the glare of the sun. Thus our artist is started; she is going to make a sketch of the after-part of the yacht with Hector of Moidart at the tiller: beyond, the calm blue seas, and a faint promontory of land.

Then the Laird—having confidentially remarked to Miss Avon that Tom Galbraith, than whom there is no greater authority living, invariably moistens the fresh canvas with megilp before beginning work—has turned to the last report of the Semple case.

"No, no," says he to our sovereign lady, who is engaged in some mysterious work in wool, "it does not look well for the Presbytery to go over every one of the charges in the major proposection—supported by the averments in the minor—only to find them irrelevant; and then bring home to him the part of the libel that deals with tendency. No, no; that shows a lamentable want of purpose. In view of the great danger to be apprehended from these secret assaults on the inspiration of the Scriptures, they should have stuck to each charge with tenaheity. Now, I will just show ye where Dr. Carnegie, in defending *Secundo*—illustrated as it was with the extracts and averments in the minor—let the whole thing slip through his fingers."

But if any one were disposed to be absolutely idle on this calm, shining, beautiful day—far away from the cares and labours of the land? Out on the taffrail, under shadow of the mizen, there is a seat that is gratefully cool. The Mare of the sea no longer bewilders the eyes; one can watch with a lazy enjoyment the teeming life of the open Atlantic. The great skarts go whizzing by, long-necked, rapid of flight. The gannets poise in the air, and then there is a sudden dart downwards, and a spout of water flashes up where the bird has dived. The guillemots fill the silence with their soft kurrooing—and here they are on all sides of us—*Kirroo! Kurroo!*—dipping their bills in the water, hastening away from the vessel, and then rising on the surface to flap their wings. But this is a strange thing: they are all in pairs—obviously mother and child—and the mother calls *Kurroo! Kurroo!*—and the young one unable as yet to dive or swim, answers *Pe-yoo-it! Pe-yoo-it!* and flutters and paddles after her. But where is the father? And has the guillemot only one of a family? Over that one, at all events, she exercises a valiant protection. Even though the stem of the yacht seems likely to run both of them down, she will neither dive nor fly until she has piloted the young one out of danger.

Then a sudden cry startles the Laird from his heresy-case and Mary Avon from her canvas. A sound far away has turned all eyes to the north; though there is nothing visible there, over the shining calm of the sea, but a small cloud of white spray that slowly sinks. In a second or two, however, we see another jet of white water arise; and then a great brown mass heave slowly over; and then we hear the spouting of the whale.

"What a huge animal!" cries one. "A hundred feet!"

"Eighty, any way!"

The whale is sheering off to the north: there is less and less chance of our forming any correct estimate.

"Oh, I am sure it was a hundred! Don't you think so, Angus?" says our admiral.

"Well," says the Doctor, slowly—pretending to be very anxious about keeping the sails full (when there was no wind)—"you know there is a great difference between 'yacht measurement' and 'registered tonnage.' A vessel of fifty registered tons may become eighty or ninety by yacht measurement. And I have often noticed," continues this graceless young man, who takes no thought how he is bringing contempt on his elders, "that objects seen from the deck of a yacht are naturally subject to 'yacht measurement.' I don't know what the size of that whale may be. Its registered tonnage, I suppose, would be the number of Jonahs it could carry. But I should think that if the apparent 'yacht measurement' was a hundred feet, the whale was probably about twenty feet long."

It was thus he tried to diminish the marvels of the deep! But, however he might crush us otherwise, we were his masters on one point. The Semple heresy-case was too deep even for him. What could he make of "*the first alternative of the general major*"?

And see now, on this calm summer evening, we pass between Muick and Eigg; and the sea is like a plain of gold. As we draw near the sombre mass of Rum, the sunset deepens, and a strange lurid mist hangs around this remote and mountainous island rising sheer from the Atlantic. Gloomy and mysterious are the vast peaks of Haleval and Haskeval; we creep under them—favoured by a flood-tide—and the silence of the desolate shores seems to spread out from them and to encompass us.

Mary Avon has long ago put away her canvas; she sits and watches; and her soft black eyes are full of dreaming as she gazes up at those thunder-dark mountains against the rosy haze of the west.

"Haleval and Haskeval?" Angus Sutherland repeats, in reply to his hostess; but he starts all the same, for he has been covertly regarding the dark and wistful eyes of the girl sitting there. "Oh, these are Norse names. Scuir na Gillean, on the other hand, is Gaelic—it is *the peak of the young men*. Perhaps, the Norsemen had the north of the island, and the Celts the south."

Whether they were named by Scandinavian or by Celt, Haleval and Haskeval seemed to overshadow us with their sultry gloom as we slowly glided into the lonely loch lying at their base. We were the only vessel there; and we could make out no sign of life on shore, until the glass revealed to us one or two half-ruined cottages. The northern twilight shone in the sky far into the night; but neither that clear metallic glow, nor any radiance from moon, or planet, or star, seemed to affect the thunder-darkness of Haskeval and Haleval's silent peaks.

There was another tale to tell below—the big saloon aglow with candles; the white table-cover with its centre-piece of roses, nasturtiums, and ferns; the delayed dinner, or supper, or whatever it might be called, all artistically arranged; our young Doctor most humbly solicitous that Mary Avon should be comfortably seated, and, in fact, quite usurping the office of the Laird in that respect; and then a sudden sound in the galley, a hissing as of a thousand squibs, telling us that Master Fred had once more and ineffectually tried to suppress the released genie of the bottle by jamming down the cork. Forthwith the Laird, with his old-fashioned ways, must needs propose a health, which is that of our most sovereign and midge-like mistress; and this he does with an elaborate and gracious and sonorous courtesy. And surely there is no reason why Mary Avon should not for once break her habit and join in that simple ceremony; especially when it is a real live Doctor—and not only a Doctor, but an encyclopædia of scientific and all other knowledge—who would fain fill her glass? Angus Sutherland timidly but seriously pleads; and he does not plead in vain; and you would think from his look that she had conferred an extraordinary favour on him. Then we—we propose a health too—the health of the FOUR WINDS! and we do not care which of them it is who is coming to-morrow, so long as he or she comes in force. Blow, breezes, blow!—from the Coolins of Skye, or the shores of Coll, or the glens of Arisaig and Moidart—for to-morrow morning we shake out once more the white wings of the *White Dove*, and set forth for the loneliness of the northern seas.

CHAPTER VIII.
PLOTS AND COUNTER-PLOTS.

Now the Laird has a habit—laudable or not—of lingering over an additional half-cup at breakfast, as an excuse for desultory talk; and thus it is, on this particular morning, the young people having gone on deck to see the yacht get under way, that Denny-mains has a chance of revealing to us certain secret schemes of his over which he has apparently been brooding. How could we have imagined that all this plotting and planning had been going on beneath the sedate exterior of the Commissioner for the Burgh of Strathgovan?

"She's just a wonderful bit lass!" he says, confidently, to his hostess; "as happy and contented as the day is long; and when she's not singing to herself, her way of speech has a sort of—a sort of music in it that is quite new to me. Yes, I must admit that; I did not know that the southern English tongue was so accurate and pleasant to the ear. Ay, but what will become of her?"

What, indeed! The lady whom he was addressing had often spoken to him of Mary Avon's isolated position in the world.

"It fairly distresses me," continues the good-hearted Laird, "when I think of her condeetion—not at present, when she has, if I may be allowed to say so, *several* friends near her who would be glad to do what they could for her; but by and by, when she is becoming older——"

The Laird hesitated. Was it possible, after all, that he was about to hint at the chance of Mary Avon becoming the mistress of the mansion and estate of Denny-mains? Then he made a plunge.

"A young woman in her position should have a husband to protect her, that is what I am sure of. Have ye never thought of it, ma'am?"

"I should like very well to see Mary married," says the other, demurely. "And I know she would make an excellent wife."

"An excellent wife!" exclaims the Laird; and then he adds, with a tone approaching to severity, "I tell ye he will be a fortunate man that gets her. Oh, ay; I have watched her. I can keep my eyes open when there is need. Did you hear her asking the captain about his wife and children? I tell you there's *human nature* in that lass."

There was no need for the Laird to be so pugnacious; we were not contesting the point. However, he resumed—

"I have been thinking," said he, with a little more shyness, "about my nephew. He's a good lad. Well, ye know, ma'am, that I do not approve of young men being brought up in idleness, whatever their prospects must be; and I have no doubt whatever that my nephew Howard is working hard enough—what with the reading of law-books, and attending the courts, and all that—though as yet he has not had much business. But then there is no necessity. I do not think he is a lad of any great ambeetion, like your friend Mr. Sutherland, who has to fight his way in the world in any case. But Howard—I have been thinking now that if he was to get married and settled, he might give up the law business altogether; and, if they were content to live in Scotland, he might look after Denny-mains. It will be his in any case, ye know; he would have the interest of a man looking after his own property. Now, I will tell ye plainly, ma'am, what I have been thinking about this day or two back; if Howard would marry your young lady friend, that would be agreeable to me."

The calm manner in which the Laird announced his scheme showed that it had been well matured. It was a natural, simple, feasible arrangement, by which two persons in whom he took a warm interest would be benefited at once.

"But then, sir," said his hostess, with a smile which she could not wholly repress, "you know people never do marry to please a third person—at least, very seldom."

"Oh, there can be no forcing," said the Laird with decision. "But I have done a great deal for Howard; may I not expect that he will do something for me?"

"Oh, doubtless, doubtless," says this amiable lady, who has had some experience in match-making herself; "but I have generally found that marriages that would be in every way suitable and pleasing to friends, and obviously desirable, are precisely the marriages that never come off. Young people, when they are flung at each other's heads, to use the common phrase, never will be sensible and please their relatives. Now if you were to bring your nephew here, do you think Mary would fall in love with him because she ought? More likely you would find that, out of pure contrariety, she would fall in love with Angus Sutherland, who cannot afford to marry, and whose head is filled with other things."

"I am not sure, I am not sure," said the Laird, musingly. "Howard is a good-looking young fellow, and a capital lad, too. I am not so sure."

"And then, you know," said the other shyly, for she will not plainly say anything to Mary's disparagement, "young men have different tastes in their choice of a wife. He might not have the high opinion of her that you have."

At this the Laird gave a look of surprise—even of resentment.

"Then I'll tell ye what it is, ma'am," said he, almost angrily; "if my nephew had the chance of marrying such a girl, and did not do so, I should consider him—I should consider him *a fool*, and say so."

And then he added, sharply—

"And do ye think I would let Denny-mains pass into the hands of *a fool?*"

Now this kind lady had had no intention of rousing the wrath of the Laird in this manner; and she instantly set about pacifying him. And the Laird was easily pacified. In a minute or two he was laughing good-naturedly at himself for getting into a passion; he said it would not do for one at his time of life to try to play the part of the stern father as they played that in theatre pieces—there was to be no forcing.

"But he's a good lad, ma'am, a good lad," said he, rising as his hostess rose; and he added, significantly, "he is no fool, I assure ye, ma'am; he has plenty of common sense."

When we get up on deck again, we find that the *White Dove* is gently gliding out of the lonely Loch Scresorst, with its solitary house among the trees, and its crofters' huts at the base of the sombre hills. And as the light cool breeze—gratefully cool after the blazing heat of the last day or two—carries us away northward, we see more and more of the awful solitudes of Haleval and Haskeval, that are still thunderous and dark under the hazy sky. Above the great shoulders, and under the purple peaks, we see the far-reaching corries opening up, with here and there a white waterfall just visible in the hollows. There is a sense of escape as we draw away from that overshadowing gloom.

Then we discover that we have a new skipper to-day, *vice* John of Skye, deposed. The fresh hand is Mary Avon, who is at the tiller, and looking exceedingly business-like. She has been promoted to this post by Dr. Sutherland, who stands by; she receives explanations about the procedure of Hector of Moidart, who is up aloft, lacing the smaller topsail to the mast; she watches the operations of John of Skye and Sandy, who are at the sheets below; and, like a wise and considerate captain, she pretends not to notice Master Fred, who is having a quiet smoke by the windlass. And so, past those lonely shores sails the brave vessel—the yawl *White Dove*, Captain Mary Avon, bound for anywhere.

But you must not imagine that the new skipper is allowed to stand by the tiller. Captain though she may be, she has to submit civilly to dictation, in so far as her foot is concerned, Our young Doctor has compelled her to be seated, and he has passed a rope round the tiller that so she can steer from her chair, and from time to time he gives suggestions, which she receives as orders.

"I wish I had been with you when you first sprained your foot," he says.

"Yes?" she answers, with humble inquiry in her eyes.

"I would have put it in plaster of Paris," he says, in a matter-of-fact way, "and locked you up in the house for a fortnight; at the end of that time you would not know which ankle was the sprained one."

There was neither "with your leave" nor "by your leave" in this young man's manner when he spoke of that accident. He would have taken possession of her. He would have discarded your bandages and hartshorn, and what not; when it was Mary Avon's foot that was concerned—it was intimated to us—he would have had his own way in spite of all comers.

"I wish I had known," she says, timidly, meaning that it was the treatment she wished she had known.

"There is a more heroic remedy," said he, with a smile; "and that is walking the sprain off. I believe that can be done, but most people would shrink from the pain. Of course, if it were done at all, it would be done by a woman; women can bear pain infinitely better than men."

"Oh, do you think so!" she says, in mild protest. "Oh, I am sure not. Men are so much braver than women, so much stronger——"

But this gentle quarrel is suddenly stopped, for some one calls attention to a deer that is calmly browsing on one of the high slopes above that rocky shore, and instantly all glasses are in request. It is a hind, with a beautifully shaped head and slender legs; she takes no notice of the passing craft, but continues her feeding, walking a few steps onward from time to time. In this way she reaches the edge of a gully in the rugged cliffs where there is some brushwood, and probably a stream; into this she sedately descends, and we see her no more.

Then there is another cry; what is this cloud ahead, or waterspout resting on the calm bosom of the sea? Glasses again in request, amid many exclamations, reveal to us that this is a dense cloud of birds; a flock so vast that towards the water it seems black; can it be the dead body of a whale that has collected this world of wings from all the Northern seas? Hurry on, *White Dove*; for the floating cloud with the black base is moving and seething—in fantastic white fumes, as it were—in the loveliness of this summer day. And now, as we draw nearer, we can descry that there is no dead body of a whale causing that blackness; but only the density of the mass of seafowl. And nearer and nearer as we draw, behold! the great gannets swooping down in such numbers that the sea is covered with a mist of waterspouts;

and the air is filled with innumerable cries; and we do not know what to make of this bewildering, fluttering, swimming, screaming mass of terns, guillemots, skarts, kittiwakes, razorbills, puffins, and gulls. But they draw away again. The herring-shoal is moving northward. The murmur of cries becomes more remote, and the seething cloud of the seabirds is slowly dispersing. When the *White Dove* sails up to the spot at which this phenomenon was first seen, there is nothing visible but a scattered assemblage of guillemots—*kurroo! kurroo!* answered by *pe-yoo-it! pe-yoo-it!*—and great gannets—"as big as a sheep," says John of Skye—apparently so gorged that they lie on the water within stone's-throw of the yacht, before spreading out their long, snow-white, black-tipped wings to bear them away over the sea.

And now, as we are altering our course to the west—far away to our right stand the vast Coolins of Skye—we sail along the northern shores of Rum. There is no trace of any habitation visible; nothing but the precipitous cliffs, and the sandy bays, and the outstanding rocks dotted with rows of shining black skarts. When Mary Avon asks why those sandy bays should be so red, and why a certain ruddy warmth of colour should shine through even the patches of grass, our F.R.S. begins to speak of powdered basalt rubbed down from the rocks above. He would have her begin another sketch, but she is too proud of her newly acquired knowledge to forsake the tiller.

The wind is now almost dead aft, and we have a good deal of gybing. Other people might think that all this gybing was an evidence of bad steering on the part of our new skipper; but Angus Sutherland—and we cannot contradict an F.R.S.—assures Miss Avon that she is doing remarkably well; and, as he stands by to lay hold of the main sheet when the boom swings over, we are not in much danger of carrying away either port or starboard davits.

"Do you know," says he lightly, "I sometimes think I ought to apply for the post of surgeon on board a man-of-war? That would just suit me——"

"Oh, I hope you will not," she blurts out quite inadvertently; and thereafter there is a deep blush on her face.

"I should enjoy it immensely, I know," says he, wholly ignorant of her embarrassment, because he is keeping an eye on the sails. "I believe I should have more pleasure in life that way than any other——"

"But you do not live for your own pleasure," says she hastily, perhaps to cover her confusion.

"I have no one else to live for, any way," says he, with a laugh; and then he corrected himself. "Oh, yes, I have. My father is a sad heretic. He has fallen away from the standards of his faith; he has set up idols—the diplomas and medals I have got from time to time. He has them all arranged in his study, and I have heard that he positively sits down before them and worships them. When I sent him the medal from Vienna—it was only bronze—he returned to me his Greek Testament, that he had interleaved and annotated when he was a student; I believe it was his greatest possession."

"And you would give up all that he expects from you to go away and be a doctor on board a ship!" says Mary Avon, with some proud emphasis. "That would not be my ambition if I were a man, and—and—if I had—if——"

Well, she could not quite say to Brose's face what she thought of his powers and prospects; so she suddenly broke away and said—

"Yes; you would go and do that for your own amusement? And what would the amusement be? Do you think they would let the doctor interfere with the sailing of the ship?"

"Well," said he, laughing, "that is a practical objection. I don't suppose the captain of a man-of-war or even of a merchant vessel would be as accommodating as your John of Skye. Captain John has his compensation when he is relieved; he can go forward, and light his pipe."

"Well, I think for *your father's sake*," says Miss Avon, with decision, "you had better put that idea out of your head, once and for all."

Now blow, breezes, blow! What is the great headland that appears, striking out into the wide Atlantic?

Ahead she goes! the land she knows!
Behold! the snowy shores of Canna!
Ho, ro, clansmen!
A long, strong pull together,
Ho, ro, clansmen!

"Tom Galbraith," the Laird is saying solemnly to his hostess, "has assured me that Rum is the most picturesque island on the whole of the western coast of Scotland. That is his deleeberate opinion. And indeed I would not go so far as to say he was wrong. Arran! They talk about Arran! Just look at those splendid mountains coming sheer down to the sea; and the light of the sun on them! Eh me, what a sunset there will be this night!"

"Canna?" says Dr. Sutherland, to his interlocutor, who seems very anxious to be instructed. "Oh, I don't know. *Canna* in Gaelic is simply a can; but then *Cana* is a whale; and the island in the distance looks long and flat on the water. Or it may be from *canach*—that is, the moss-cotton; or from *cannach*—that is, the sweet-gale. You see, Miss Avon, ignorant people have an ample choice."

Blow! breezes blow! as the yellow light of the afternoon shines over the broad Atlantic. Here are the eastern shores of Canna, high and rugged, and dark with caves; and there the western shores of Rum, the mighty mountains aglow in the evening light. And this remote and solitary little bay, with its green headlands, and its awkward rocks at the mouth, and the one house presiding over it amongst that shining wilderness of shrubs and flowers? Here is fair shelter for the night.

After dinner, in the lambent twilight, we set out with the gig; and there was much preparation of elaborate contrivances for the entrapping of fish. But the Laird's occult and intricate tackle—the spinning minnows, and spoons, and india-rubber sand-eels—proved no competitor for the couple of big white flies that Angus Sutherland had busked. And of course Mary Avon had that rod; and when some huge lithe dragged the end of the rod fairly under water, and when she cried aloud, "Oh! oh! I can't hold it; he'll break the rod!" then arose our Doctor's word of command:—

"Haul him in! Shove out the butt! No scientific playing with a lithe! Well done!—well done!—a five-pounder I'll bet ten farthings!"

It was not scientific fishing; but we got big fish—which is of more importance in the eyes of Master Fred. And then, as the night fell, we set out again for the yacht; and the Doctor pulled stroke; and he sang some more verses of the *biorlinn* song as the blades dashed fire into the rushing sea:—

Proudly o'er the waves we'll bound her,
As the staghound bounds the heather!
Ho, ro, clansmen!
A long, strong pull together,
Ho, ro, clansmen!

Through the eddying tide we'll guide her,
Round each isle and breezy headland,
Ho, ro, clansmen!
A long, strong pull together,
Ho, ro, clansmen!

The yellow lamp at the bow of the yacht grew larger and larger; the hull of the boat looked black between us and the starlit heavens; as we clambered on board there was a golden glow from the saloon skylight. And then, during the long and happy evening, amid all the whist-playing and other amusements going forward, what about certain timid courtesies and an occasional shy glance between those two young people? Some of us began to think that if the Laird's scheme was to come to anything, it was high time that Mr. Howard Smith put in an appearance.

CHAPTER IX.
A WILD STUDIO.

There is a fine bustle of preparation next morning—for the gig is waiting by the side of the yacht; and Dr. Sutherland is carefully getting our artist's materials into the stern; and the Laird is busy with shawls and waterproofs; and Master Fred brings along the luncheon-basket. Our Admiral-in-chief prefers to stay on board; she has letters to write; there are enough of us to go and be tossed on the Atlantic swell off the great caves of Canna.

And as the men strike their oars in the water and we wave a last adieu, the Laird catches a glimpse of our larder at the stern of the yacht. Alas! there is but one remaining piece of fresh meat hanging there, under the white canvas.

"It reminds me," says he, beginning to laugh already, "of a good one that Tom Galbraith told me—a real good one that was. Tom had a little bit yacht that his man and himself sailed when he was painting, ye know; and one day they got into a bay where Duncan—that was the man's name—had some friends ashore. Tom left him in charge of the yacht; and—and—ha! ha! ha!—there was a leg of mutton hanging at the stern. Well, Tom was rowed ashore; and painted all day; and came back to the yacht in the afternoon. *There was no leg of mutton*! 'Duncan,' says he, 'where is the leg of mutton?' Duncan pretended to be vastly surprised. 'Iss it away?' says he. 'Away?' says Tom. 'Don't you see it is away? I want to know who took it!' Duncan looked all round him—at the sea and the sky—and then says he—then says he, 'Maybe it wass a dog!'—ha! ha! hee! hee! hee!—'maybe it wass a dog,' says he; and they were half a mile from the shore! I never see the canvas at the stern of a yacht without thinking o' Tom Galbraith and the leg of mutton;" and here the Laird laughed long and loud again.

"I have heard you speak once or twice about Tom Galbraith," remarked our young Doctor, without meaning the least sarcasm; "he is an artist, I suppose?"

The Laird stopped laughing. There was a look of indignant wonder—approaching to horror—on his face. But when he proceeded, with some dignity and even resentment, to explain to this ignorant person the immense importance of the school that Tom Galbraith had been chiefly instrumental in forming; and the high qualities of that artist's personal work; and how the members of the Royal Academy shook in their shoes at the mere mention of Tom Galbraith's name, he became more pacified; for Angus Sutherland listened with great respect, and even promised to look out for Mr. Galbraith's work if he passed through Edinburgh on his way to the south.

The long, swinging stroke of the men soon took us round the successive headlands until we were once more in the open, with the mountains of Skye in the north, and, far away at the horizon, a pale line which we knew to be North Uist. And now the green shores of Canna were becoming more precipitous; and there was a roaring of the sea along the spurs of black rock; and the long Atlantic swell, breaking on the bows of the gig, was sending a little more spray over us than was at all desirable. Certainly no one who could have seen the Doctor at this moment—with his fresh-coloured face dripping with the salt water and shining in the sunlight—would have taken him for a hard-worked and anxious student. His hard work was pulling stroke-oar, and he certainly put his shoulders into it, as the Laird had remarked; and his sole anxiety was about Mary Avon's art-materials. That young lady shook the water from the two blank canvases, and declared it did not matter a bit.

These lonely cliffs!—becoming more grim and awful every moment, as this mite of a boat still wrestles with the great waves, and makes its way along the coast. And yet there are tender greens where the pasturage appears on the high plateaus; and there is a soft ruddy hue where the basalt shines. The gloom of the picture appears below—in the caves washed out of the conglomerate by the heavy seas; in the spurs and fantastic pillars and arches of the black rock; and in this leaden-hued Atlantic springing high over every obstacle to go roaring and booming into the caverns. And these innumerable white specks on the sparse green plateaus and on this high promontory: can they be mushrooms in millions? Suddenly one of the men lifts his oar from the rowlock, and rattles it on the gunwale of the gig. At this sound a cloud rises from the black rocks; it spreads; the next moment the air is darkened over our heads; and almost before we know what has happened, this vast multitude of puffins has wheeled by us, and wheeled again further out to sea—a smoke of birds! And as we watch them, behold! stragglers come back—in thousands upon thousands—the air is filled with them—some of them swooping so near us that we can see the red parrot-like beak and the orange-hued web-feet, and then again the green shelves of grass and the pinnacles of rock become dotted with those white specks. The myriads of birds; the black caverns; the arches and spurs of rock; the leaden-hued Atlantic bounding and springing in white foam: what says Mary Avon to that? Has she the courage?

"If you can put me ashore?" says she.

"Oh, we will get you ashore, somehow," Dr. Sutherland answers.

But, indeed, the nearer we approach that ugly coast the less we like the look of it. Again and again we make for what should be a sheltered bit; but long before we can get to land we can see through the plunging sea great masses of yellow, which we know to be the barnacled rock; and then ahead we find a shore that, in this heavy surf, would make matchwood of the gig in three seconds. Our Doctor, however, will not give in. If he cannot get the gig on to any beach or into any creek, he will land our artist somehow. And at last—and in spite of the remonstrances of John of Skye—he insists on having the boat backed in to a projecting mass of conglomerate, all yellowed over with small shell-fish, against which the sea is beating heavily. It is an ugly landing-place; we can see the yellow rock go sheer down in the clear green sea; and the surf is spouting up the side in white jets. But if she can watch a high wave, and put her foot there—and there—will she not find herself directly on a plateau of rock at least twelve feet square?

"Back her, John!—back her!—" and therewith the Doctor, watching his chance, scrambles out and up to demonstrate the feasibility of the thing. And the easel is handed out to him; and the palette and canvases; and finally Mary Avon herself. Nay, even the Laird will adventure, sending on before him the luncheon-basket.

It is a strange studio—this projecting shell-crusted rock, surrounded on three sides by the sea, and on the fourth by an impassable cliff. And the sounds beneath our feet—there must be some subterranean passage or cave into which the sea roars and booms. But Angus Sutherland rigs up the easel rapidly; and arranges the artist's camp-stool; and sets her fairly agoing; then he proposes to leave the Laird in charge of her. He and the humble chronicler of the adventures of these people mean to have some further exploration of this wild coast.

But we had hardly gone a quarter of a mile or so—it was hard work pulling in this heavy sea—when the experienced eye of Sandy from Islay saw that something was wrong.

"What's that?" he said, staring.

We turned instantly, and strove to look through the mists of spray. Where we had left the Laird and Mary Avon there were now visible only two mites, apparently not bigger than puffins. But is not one of the puffins gesticulating wildly?

"Round with her, John!" the Doctor calls out. "They want us—I'm sure."

And away the gig goes again—plunging into the great troughs and then swinging up to the giddy crests. And as we get nearer and nearer, what is the meaning of the Laird's frantic gestures? We cannot understand him; and it is impossible to hear, for the booming of the sea into the caves drowns his voice.

"He has lost his hat," says Angus Sutherland; and then, the next second, "Where's the easel?"

Then we understand those wild gestures. Pull away, merry men! for has not a squall swept the studio of its movables? And there, sure enough, tossing high and low on the waves, we descry a variety of things—an easel, two canvases, a hat, a veil, and what not. Up with the boat-hook to the bow; and gently with those plunges, you eager Hector of Moidart!

"I am so sorry," she says (or rather shrieks), when her dripping property is restored to her.

"It was my fault," our Doctor yells; "but I will undertake to fasten your easel properly this time"—and therewith he fetches a lump of rock that might have moored a man-of-war.

We stay and have luncheon in this gusty and thunderous studio—though Mary Avon will scarcely turn from her canvas. And there is no painting of pink geraniums about this young woman's work. We see already that she has got a thorough grip of this cold, hard coast (the sun is obscured now, and the various hues are more sombre than ever); and, though she has not had time as yet to try to catch the motion of the rolling sea, she has got the colour of it—a leaden-grey, with glints of blue and white, and with here and there a sudden splash of deep, rich, glassy, bottle green, where some wave for a moment catches, just as it gets to the shore, a reflection from the grass plateaus above. Very good, Miss Avon; very good—but we pretend that we are not looking.

Then away we go again, to leave the artist to her work; and we go as near as possible—the high sea will not allow us to enter—the vast black caverns; and we watch through the clear water for those masses of yellow rock. And then the multitudes of white-breasted, red-billed birds perched up there—close to the small burrows in the scant grass; they jerk their heads about in a watchful way just like the prairie-dogs at the mouth of their sandy habitations on the Colorado plains. And then again a hundred or two of them come swooping down from the rocky pinnacles and sail over our heads—twinkling bits of colour between the grey-green sea and the blue-and-white of the sky. They resent the presence of strangers in this far-home of the sea-birds.

It is a terrible business getting that young lady and her paraphernalia back into the gig again; for the sea is still heavy, and, of course, additional care has now to be taken of the precious canvas. But at last she, and the Laird, and the luncheon-basket, and everything else have been got on board; and away we go for the yacht again, in the now clearing afternoon. As we draw further away from the roar of the caves, it is more feasible to talk; and naturally we are all very complimentary about Mary Avon's sketch in oils.

"Ay," says the Laird, "and it wants but one thing; and I am sure I could get Tom Galbraith to put that in for you. A bit of a yacht, ye know, or other sailing vessel, put below the cliffs, would give people a notion of the height of the cliffs, do ye see? I am sure I could get Tom Galbraith to put that in for ye."

"I hope Miss Avon won't let Tom Galbraith or anybody else meddle with the picture." says Angus Sutherland, with some emphasis. "Why, a yacht! Do you think anybody would let a yacht come close to rocks like these! As soon as you introduce any making-up like that, the picture is a sham. It is the real thing now, as it stands. Twenty years hence you could take up that piece of canvas, and there before you would be the very day that you spent here—it would be like finding your old life of twenty years before opened up to you with a lightning-flash. The picture is—why I should say it is invaluable, as it stands."

At this somewhat fierce praise, Mary Avon colours a little. And then she says with a gentle hypocrisy—

"Oh, do you really think there is—there is—some likeness to the place?"

"It is the place itself!" says he warmly.

"Because," she says, timidly, and yet with a smile, "one likes to have one's work appreciated, however stupid it may be. And—and—if you think that—would you like to have it? Because I should be so proud if you would take it—only I am ashamed to offer my sketches to anybody——"

"That!" said he, staring at the canvas as if the mines of Golconda were suddenly opened to him. But then he drew back. "Oh, no," he said; "you are very kind—but—but, you know, I cannot. You would think I had been asking for it."

"Well," says Miss Avon, still looking down, "I never was treated like this before. You won't take it? You don't think it is worth putting in your portmanteau?"

At this the young Doctor's face grew very red; but he said boldly—

"Very well, now, if you have been playing fast and loose, you shall be punished. I *will* take the picture, whether you grudge it me or not. And I don't mean to give it up now."

"Oh," said she, very gently, "if it reminds you of the place, I shall be very pleased—and—and it may remind you too that I am not likely to forget your kindness to poor Mrs. Thompson."

And so this little matter was amicably settled—though the Laird looked with a covetous eye on that rough sketch of the rocks of Canna, and regretted that he was not to be allowed to ask Tom Galbraith to put in a touch or two. And so back to the yacht, and to dinner in the silver clear evening; and how beautiful looked this calm bay of Canna, with its glittering waters and green shores, after the grim rocks and the heavy Atlantic waves!

That evening we pursued the innocent lithe again—our larder was becoming terribly empty—and there was a fine take. But of more interest to some of us than the big fish was the extraordinary wonder of colour in sea and sky when the sun had gone down; and there was a wail on the part of the Laird that Mary Avon had not her colours with her to put down some jotting for further use. Or if on paper: might not she write down something of what she saw; and experiment thereafter? Well, if any artist can make head or tail of words in such a case as this, here they are for him—as near as our combined forces of observation could go.

The vast plain of water around us a blaze of salmon-red—with the waves (catching the reflection of the zenith) marked in horizontal lines of blue. The great headland of Canna, between us and the western sky, a mass of dark, intense olive-green. The sky over that a pale, clear lemon-yellow. But the great feature of this evening scene was a mass of cloud that stretched all across the heavens—a mass of flaming, thunderous, orange-red cloud that began in the far pale mists in the east, and came across the blue zenith overhead, burning with a splendid glory there, and then stretched over to the west, where it narrowed down and was lost in the calm, clear gold of the horizon. The splendour of this great cloud was bewildering to the eyes; one turned gratefully to the reflection of it in the sultry red of the sea below, broken by the blue lines of waves. Our attention was not wholly given to the fishing or the boat on this lambent evening; perhaps that was the reason we ran on a rock, and with difficulty got off again.

Then back to the yacht again about eleven o'clock. What is this terrible news from Master Fred, who was sent off with instructions to hunt up any stray crofter he might find, and use such persuasions in the shape of Gaelic friendliness and English money as would enable us to replenish our larder? What! that he had walked two miles and seen nothing eatable or purchasable but an old hen? Canna is a beautiful place; but we begin to think it is time to be off.

On this still night, with the stars coming out, we cannot go below. We sit on deck and listen to the musical whisper along the shore, and watch one golden-yellow planet rising over the dusky peaks of Rum, far in the east. And our young Doctor is talking of the pathetic notices that are common in the Scotch papers—in the advertisements of deaths. "*New Zealand papers, please copy.*" "*Canadian papers, please copy.*" When you see this prayer appended to the announcement of the death of some old woman of seventy or seventy-five, do you not know that it is a message to loved ones in distant climes, wanderers who may forget but who have not been forgotten? They are messages that tell of a scattered race—of a race that once filled the glens of these now almost deserted islands. And surely, when some birthday or other time of recollection comes round, those far away,

Where wild Altama murmurs to their woe,

must surely bethink themselves of the old people left behind—living in Glasgow or Greenock now, perhaps—and must bethink themselves too of the land where last they saw the bonny red heather, and where last they heard the pipes playing the sad *Farewell, MacCruimin* as the ship stood out to sea. They cannot quite forget the scenes of their youth—the rough seas and the red heather and the islands; the wild dancing at the weddings; the secret meetings in the glen, with Ailasa, or Morag, or Mairi, come down from the sheiling, all alone, a shawl round her head to shelter her from the rain, her heart fluttering like the heart of a timid fawn. They cannot forget.

And we, too, we are going away; and it may be that we shall never see this beautiful bay or the island there again. But one of us carries away with him a talisman for the sudden revival of old memories. And twenty years hence—that was his own phrase—what will Angus Sutherland—perhaps a very great and rich person by that time—what will he think when he turns to a certain picture, and recalls the long summer day when he rowed with Mary Avon round the wild shores of Canna?

CHAPTER X.
"DUNVEGAN!—OH! DUNVEGAN!"

Commander Mary Avon sends her orders below: everything to be made snug in the cabins, for there is a heavy sea running outside, and the *White Dove* is already under way. Farewell, then, you beautiful blue bay—all rippled into silver now with the breeze—and green shores and picturesque cliffs! We should have lingered here another day or two, perhaps, but for the report about that one old hen. We cannot ration passengers and crew on one old hen.

And here, as we draw away from Canna, is the vast panorama of the sea-world around us once more—the mighty mountain range of Skye shining faintly in the northern skies; Haleval and Haskeval still of a gloomy purple in the east; and away beyond these leagues of rushing Atlantic the clear blue line of North Uist. Whither are we bound, then, you small captain with the pale face and the big, soft, tender black eyes? Do you fear a shower of spray that you have strapped that tightly-fitting ulster round the graceful small figure? And are you quite sure that you know whether the wind is on the port or starboard beam?

"Look! look! look!" she calls, and our F.R.S., who has been busy over the charts, jumps to his feet.

Just at the bow of the vessel we see the great shining black thing disappear. What if there had been a collision?

"You cannot call *that* a porpoise, any way," says she. "Why, it must have been eighty feet long!"

"Yes, yacht measurement," says he. "But it had a back fin, which is suspicious, and it did not blow. Now," he adds—for we have been looking all round for the re-appearance of the huge stranger—"if you want to see real whales at work, just look over there, close under Rum. I should say there was a whole shoal of them in the Sound."

And there, sure enough, we see from time to time the white spoutings—rising high into the air in the form of the letter V, and slowly falling again. They are too far away for us to hear the sound of their blowing, nor can we catch any glimpse, through the best of our glasses, of their appearance at the surface. Moreover, the solitary stranger that nearly ran against our bows makes no reappearance; he has had enough of the wonders of the upper world for a time.

It is a fine sailing morning, and we pay but little attention to the fact that the wind, as usual, soon gets to be dead ahead. So long as the breeze blows, and the sun shines, and the white spray flies from the bows of the *White Dove*, what care we which harbour is to shelter us for the night? And if we cannot get into any harbour, what then? We carry our own kingdom with us; and we are far from being dependent on the one old hen.

But in the midst of much laughing at one of the Laird's good ones—the inexhaustible Homesh was again to the fore—a head appears at the top of the companion-way; and there is a respectful silence. Unseemly mirth dies away before the awful dignity of this person.

"Angus," she says, with a serious remonstrance on her face, "do you believe what scientific people tell you?"

Angus Sutherland starts, and looks up; he has been deep in a chart of Loch Bracadaile.

"Don't they say that water finds its own level? Now do you call this water finding its own level?"—and as she propounds this conundrum, she clings on tightly to the side of the companion, for, in truth, the *White Dove* is curveting a good deal among those great masses of waves.

"Another tumbler broken!" she exclaims. "Now who left that tumbler on the table?"

"I know," says Mary Avon.

"Who was it then?" says the occupant of the companion-way; and we begin to tremble for the culprit.

"Why, you yourself!"

"Mary Avon, how can you tell such a story!" says the other, with a stern face.

"Oh, but that is so," calls out our Doctor, "for I myself saw you bring the tumbler out of the ladies' cabin with water for the flowers."

The universal shout of laughter that overwhelms Madame Dignity is too much for her. A certain conscious, lurking smile begins to break through the sternness of her face.

"I don't believe a word of it," she declares, firing a shot as she retreats. "Not a word of it. You are two conspirators. To tell such a story about a tumbler——!"

But at this moment a further assault is made on the majesty of this imperious small personage. There is a thunder at the bows; a rattling as of pistol-shots on the decks forward; and at the same moment the fag-ends of the spray come flying over the after part of the yacht. What becomes of one's dignity when one gets a shower of salt water over one's head and neck? Go down below, madam!—retreat, retreat, discomfited!—go, dry your face and your bonny brown hair—and bother us no more with your broken tumbler!

And despite those plunging seas and the occasional showers of spray, Mary Avon still clings bravely to the rope that is round the tiller; and as we are bearing over for Skye on one long tack, she has no need to change her position. And if from time to time her face gets wet with the salt water, is it not quickly dried again in the warm sun and the breeze? Sun and salt water and sea-air will soon chase away the pallor from that gentle face: cannot one observe already—after only a few days' sailing—a touch of sun-brown on her cheeks?

And now we are drawing nearer and nearer to Skye, and before us lies the lonely Loch Breatal, just under the splendid Coolins. See how the vast slopes of the mountains appear to come sheer down to the lake; and there is a soft, sunny green on them—a beautiful, tender, warm colour that befits a summer day. But far above and beyond those sunny slopes a different sight appears. All the clouds of this fair day have gathered round the upper portions of the mountains; and that solitary range of black and jagged peaks is dark in shadow, dark as if with the expectation of thunder. The Coolins are not beloved of mariners. Those beautiful sunlit ravines are the secret haunts of hurricanes that suddenly come out to strike the unwary yachtsman as with the blow of a hammer. *Stand by, forward, then, lads! About ship! Down with the helm, Captain Avon!*—and behold! we are sailing away from the black Coolins, and ahead of us there is only the open sea, and the sunlight shining on the far cliffs of Canna.

"When your course is due north," remarks Angus Sutherland, who has relieved Mary Avon at the helm, "and when the wind is due north, you get a good deal of sailing for your money."

The profound truth of this remark becomes more and more apparent as the day passes in a series of long tacks which do not seem to be bringing those far headlands of Skye much nearer to us. And if we are beating in this heavy sea all day and night, is there not a chance of one or other of our women-folk collapsing? They are excellent sailors, to be sure—but—but—

Dr. Sutherland is consulted. Dr. Sutherland's advice is prompt and emphatic. His sole and only precaution against sea-sickness is simple: resolute eating and drinking. Cure for sea-sickness, after it has set in, he declares there is none: to prevent it, eat and drink, and let the drink be *brut* champagne. So our two prisoners are ordered below to undergo that punishment.

And, perhaps, it is the *brut* champagne, or perhaps it is merely the snugness of our little luncheon-party that prompts Miss Avon to remark on the exceeding selfishness of yachting and to suggest a proposal that fairly takes away our breath by its audacity.

"Now," she says, cheerfully, "I could tell you how you could occupy an idle day on board a yacht so that you would give a great deal of happiness—quite a shock of delight—to a large number of people."

Well, we are all attention.

"At what cost?" says the financier of our party.

"At no cost."

This is still more promising. Why should not we instantly set about making all those people happy?

"All that you have got to do is to get a copy of the *Field* or of the *Times* or some such paper."

Yes; and how are we to get any such thing? Rum has no post-office. No mail calls at Canna. Newspapers do not grow on the rocks of Loch Bracadaile.

"However, let us suppose that we have the paper."

"Very well. All you have to do is to sit down and take the advertisements, and write to the people, accepting all their offers on their own terms. The man who wants 500*l.* for his shooting in the autumn; the man who will sell his steam-yacht for 7,000*l,*; the curate who will take in another youth to board at 200*l.* a year; the lady who wants to let her country-house during the London season; all the people who are anxious to sell things. You offer to take them all. If a man has a yacht to let on hire, you will pay for new jerseys for the men. If a man has a house to be let, you will take all the fixtures at his own valuation. All you have to do is to write two or three hundred letters—as an anonymous person, of course—and you make two or three hundred people quite delighted for perhaps a whole week!"

The Laird stared at this young lady as if she had gone mad; but there was only a look of complacent friendliness on Mary Avon's face.

"You mean that you write sham letters?" says her hostess. "You gull those unfortunate people into believing that all their wishes are realised?"

"But you make them happy!" says Mary Avon, confidently.

"Yes—and the disappointment afterwards!" retorts her friend, almost with indignation. "Imagine their disappointment when they find they have been duped! Of course they would write letters and discover that the anonymous person had no existence."

"Oh, no!" says Mary Avon, eagerly. "There could be no such great disappointment. The happiness would be definite and real for the time. The disappointment would only be a slow and gradual thing when they found no answer coming to their letter. You would make them happy for a whole week or so by accepting their offer; whereas by not answering their letter or letters you would only puzzle them, and the matter would drop away into forgetfulness. Do you not think it would be an excellent scheme?"

Come on deck, you people; this girl has got demented. And behold! as we emerge once more into the sunlight and whirling spray and wind, we find that we are nearing Skye again on the port tack, and now it is the mouth of Loch Bracadaile that we are approaching. And these pillars of rock, outstanding from the cliffs, and worn by the northern seas?

"Why, these must be Macleod's Maidens!" says Angus Sutherland, unrolling one of the charts.

And then he discourses to us of the curious fancies of sailors—passing the lonely coasts from year to year—and recognising as old friends, not any living thing, but the strange conformations of the rocks—and giving to these the names of persons and of animals. And he thinks there is something more weird and striking about these solitary and sea-worn rocks fronting the great Atlantic than about any comparatively modern Sphinx or Pyramid; until we regard the sunlit pillars, and their fretted surface and their sharp shadows, with a sort of morbid imagination; and we discover how the sailors have fancied them to be stone women; and we see in the largest of them—her head and shoulder tilted over a bit—some resemblance to the position of the Venus discovered at Milo. All this is very fine; but suddenly the sea gets darkened over there; a squall comes roaring out of Loch Bracadaile; John of Skye orders the boat about; and presently we are running free before this puff from the north-east. Alas! alas! we have no sooner got out of the reach of the squall than the wind backs to the familiar north, and our laborious beating has to be continued as before.

But we are not discontented. Is it not enough, as the golden and glowing afternoon wears on, to listen to the innocent prattle of Denny-mains, whose mind has been fired by the sight of those pillars of rock. He tells us a great many remarkable things—about the similarity between Gaelic and Irish, and between Welsh and Armorican; and he discusses the use of the Druidical stones, as to whether the priests followed serpent-worship or devoted those circles to human sacrifice. He tells us about the Picts and Scots; about Fingal and Ossian; about the doings of Arthur in his kingdom of Strathclyde. It is a most innocent sort of prattle.

"Yes, sir," says our Doctor—quite gravely—though we are not quite sure that he is not making fun of our simple-hearted Laird, "there can be no doubt that the Aryan race that first swept over Europe spoke a Celtic language, more or less akin to Gaelic, and that they were pushed out, by successive waves of population, into Brittany, and Wales, and Ireland, and the Highlands. And I often wonder whether it was they themselves that modestly call themselves the foreigners or strangers, and affixed that name to the land they laid hold of, from Galicia and Gaul to Galloway and Galway? The Gaelic word *gall*, a stranger, you find everywhere. Fingal himself is only *Fionn-gall*—the Fair Stranger; *Dubh-gall*—that is, the familiar Dugald—or the Black Stranger—is what the Islay people call a Lowlander. *Ru-na-Gaul*, that we passed the other day—that is the Foreigner's Point. I think there can be no doubt that the tribes that first brought Aryan civilisation through the west of Europe spoke Gaelic or something like Gaelic."

"Ay," said the Laird, doubtfully. He was not sure of this young man. He had heard something about Gaelic being spoken in the Garden of Eden, and suspected there might be a joke lying about somewhere.

However, there was no joking about our F.R.S. when he began to tell Mary Avon how, if he had time and sufficient interest in such things, he would set to work to study the Basque people and their language—that strange remnant of the old race who inhabited the west of Europe long before Scot, or Briton, or Roman, or Teuton had made his appearance on the scene. Might they not have traditions, or customs, or verbal survivals to tell us of their pre-historic forefathers? The Laird seemed quite shocked to hear that his favourite Picts and Scots—and Fingal and Arthur and all the rest of them—were mere modern interlopers. What of the mysterious race that occupied these islands before the great Aryan tide swept over from the East?

Well, this was bad enough; but when the Doctor proceeded to declare his conviction that no one had the least foundation for the various conjectures about the purposes of those so-called Druidical stones—that it was all a matter of guess-work whether as regarded council-halls, grave-stones, altars, or serpent-worship—and that it was quite possible these stones were erected by the non-Aryan race who inhabited Europe before either Gaul or Roman or Teuton came west, the Laird interrupted him, triumphantly—

"But," says he, "the very names of those stones show they are of Celtic origin—will ye dispute that? What is the meaning of *Carnac*, that is in Brittany—eh? Ye know Gaelic?"

"Well, I know that much," said Angus, laughing. "Carnac means simply the place of piled stones. But the Celts may have found the stones there, and given them that name."

"I think," says Miss Avon, profoundly, "that when you go into a question of names, you can prove anything. And I suppose Gaelic is as accommodating as any other language."

Angus Sutherland did not answer for a moment; but at last he said, rather shyly—

"Gaelic is a very complimentary language, at all events. Beau is 'a woman;' and beannachd is 'a blessing.' *An ti a bheannaich thu*—that is, 'the one who blessed you.'"

Very pretty; only we did not know how wildly the young man might not be falsifying Gaelic grammar in order to say something nice to Mary Avon.

Patience works wonders. Dinner-time finds us so far across the Minch that we can make out the lighthouse of South Uist. And all these outer Hebrides are now lying in a flood of golden-red light; and on the cliffs of Canna, far away in the south-east, and now dwarfed so that they lie like a low wall on the sea, there is a paler red, caught from the glare of the sunset. And here is the silver tinkle of Master Fred's bell.

On deck after dinner; and the night air is cooler now; and there are cigars about; and our young F.R.S. is at the tiller; and Mary Avon is singing, apparently to herself, something about a Berkshire farmer's daughter. The darkness deepens, and the stars come out; and there is one star—larger than the rest, and low down, and burning a steady red—that we know to be Ushinish lighthouse. And then from time to time the silence is broken by, "*Stand by, forrard! 'Bout ship!*" and there is a rattling of blocks and cordage and then the head-sails fill and away she goes again on the other tack. We have got up to the long headlands of Skye at last.

Clear as the night is, the wind still comes in squalls, and we have the topsail down. Into which indentation of that long, low line of dark land shall we creep in the darkness?

But John of Skye keeps away from the land. It is past midnight. There is nothing visible but the black sea and the clear sky, and the red star of the lighthouse; nothing audible but Mary Avon's humming to herself and her friend—the two women sit arm-in-arm under half-a-dozen of rugs—some old-world ballad to the monotonous accompaniment of the passing seas.

One o'clock: Ushinish light is smaller now, a minute point of red fire, and the black line of land on our right looms larger in the dusk. Look at the splendour of the phosphorous-stars on the rushing waves.

And at last John of Skye says in an undertone to Angus—

"Will the leddies be going below now?"

"Going below!" he says in reply. "They are waiting till we get to anchor. We must be just off Dunvegan Loch now."

Then John of Skye makes his confession.

"Oh, yes; I been into Dunvegan Loch more as two or three times; but I not like the dark to be with us in going in; and if we lie off till the daylight comes, the leddies they can go below to their peds. And if Dr. Sutherland himself would like to see the channel in going in, will I send below when the daylight comes?"

"No, no, John; thank you," is the answer. "When I turn in, I turn in for good. I will leave you to find out the channel for yourself."

And so there is a clearance of the deck, and rugs and camp-stools handed down the companion. *Deoch-an-doruis* in the candle-lit saloon? To bed—to bed!

It is about five o'clock in the morning that the swinging out of the anchor-chain causes the yacht to tremble from stem to stern; and the sleepers start in their sleep, but are vaguely aware that they are at a safe anchorage at last. And do you know where the brave *White Dove* is lying now? Surely if the new dawn brings any stirring of wind—and if there is a sound coming over to us from this far land of legend and romance—it is the wild, sad wail of Dunvegan! The mists are clearing from the hills; the day breaks wan and fair; the great grey castle, touched by the early sunlight, looks down on the murmuring sea. And is it the sea, or is it the cold wind of the morning, that sings and sings to us in our dreams—

Dunvegan—oh! Dunvegan!

CHAPTER XI.
DRAWING NEARER.

She is all alone on deck. The morning sun shines on the beautiful blue bay; on the great castle perched on the rocks over there; and on the wooded green hills beyond. She has got a canvas fixed on her easel; she sings to herself as she works.

Now this English young lady must have beguiled the tedium of her long nursing in Edinburgh by making a particular acquaintance with Scotch ballads; or how otherwise could we account for her knowledge of the "Song of Ulva," and now of the "Song of Dunvegan?"

Macleod the faithful, and fearing none!
Dunvegan—oh! Dunvegan!

—she hums to herself as she is busy with this rough sketch of sea and shore. How can she be aware that Angus Sutherland is at this very moment in the companion way, and not daring to stir hand or foot lest he should disturb her?

Friends and foes had our passion thwarted,

she croons to herself, though, indeed, there is no despair at all in her voice, but a perfect contentment—

But true, tender, and lion-hearted,
Lived he on, and from life departed,
Macleod, whose rival is breathing none!
Dunvegan—oh, Dunvegan!

She is pleased with the rapidity of her work. She tries to whistle a little bit. Or, perhaps it is only the fresh morning air that has put her in such good spirits?

Yestreen the Queen had four Maries.

What has that got to do with the sketch of the shining grey castle? Among these tags and ends of ballads, the young Doctor at last becomes emboldened to put in an appearance.

"Good morning, Miss Avon," says he; "you are busy at work again?"

She is not in the least surprised. She has got accustomed to his coming on deck before the others; they have had a good deal of quiet chatting while as yet the Laird was only adjusting his high white collar and satin neckcloth.

"It is only a sketch," said she, in a rapid and highly business-like fashion, "but I think I shall be able to sell it. You know most people merely value pictures for their association with things they are interested in themselves. A Yorkshire farmer would rather have a picture of his favourite cob than any Raphael or Titian. And the ordinary English squire: I am sure that you know in his own heart he prefers one of Herring's farm yard pieces to Leonardo's *Last Supper*. Well, if some yachting gentleman, who has been in this loch, should see this sketch, he will probably buy it, however bad it is, just because it interests him——"

"But you don't really mean to sell it?" said he.

"That depends," said she demurely, "on whether I get any offer for it."

"Why," he exclaimed, "the series of pictures you are now making should be an invaluable treasure to you all your life long: a permanent record of a voyage that you seem to enjoy very much. I almost shrink from robbing you of that one of Canna; still, the temptation is too great. And you propose to sell them all?"

"What I can sell of them," she says; and then she adds, rather shyly, "You know I could not very well afford to keep them all for myself. I—I have a good many almoners in London; and I devote to them what I can get for my scrawls—that is, I deduct the cost of the frames, and keep the rest for them. It is not a large sum."

"Any other woman would spend it in jewellery and dresses," says he bluntly.

At this, Miss Mary Avon flushes slightly, and hastily draws his attention to a small boat that is approaching. Dr. Sutherland does not pay any heed to the boat.

He is silent for a second or so; and then he says, with an effort to talk in a cheerful and matter-of-fact way—

"You have not sent ashore yet this morning: don't you know there is a post-office at Dunvegan?"

"Oh, yes; I heard so. But the men are below at breakfast, I think, and I am in no hurry to send, for there won't be any letters for me, I know."

"Oh, indeed," he says, with seeming carelessness, "it must be a long time since you have heard from your friends."

"I have not many friends to hear from," she answers, with a light laugh, "and those I have don't trouble me with many letters. I suppose they think I am in very good hands at present."

"Oh, yes—no doubt," says he, and suddenly he begins to talk in warm terms of the delightfulness of the voyage. He is quite charmed with the appearance of Dunvegan Loch and castle. A more beautiful morning he never saw. And in the midst of all this enthusiasm the small boat comes alongside.

There is an old man in the boat, and when he has fastened his oars, he says a few words to Angus Sutherland, and hands up a big black bottle. Our young Doctor brings the bottle over to Mary Avon. He seems to be very much pleased with everything this morning.

"Now, is not that good-natured?" says he. "It is a bottle of fresh milk, with the compliments of ———, of Uginish. Isn't it good-natured?"

"Oh, indeed it is," says she, plunging her hand into her pocket. "You must let me give the messenger half-a-crown."

"No, no; that is not the Highland custom," says the Doctor; and therewith he goes below, and fetches up another black bottle, and pours out a glass of whiskey with his own hand, and presents it to the ancient boatman. You should have seen the look of surprise in the old man's face when Angus Sutherland said something to him in the Gaelic.

And alas! and alas!—as we go ashore on this beautiful bright day, we have to give up for ever the old Dunvegan of many a dream—the dark and solitary keep that we had imagined perched high above the Atlantic breakers—the sheer precipices, the awful sterility, the wail of lamentation along the lonely shores. This is a different picture altogether that Mary Avon has been trying to put down on her canvas—a spacious, almost modern-looking, but nevertheless picturesque castle, sheltered from the winds by softly wooded hills, a bit of smooth, blue water below, and further along the shores the cheerful evidences of fertility and cultivation. The wail of Dunvegan? Why, here is a brisk and thriving village, with a post-office, and a shop, and a building that looks uncommonly like an inn; and there, dotted all about, and encroaching on the upper moorland, any number of those small crofts that were once the pride of the Highlands and that gave to England the most stalwart of her regiments. Here are no ruined huts and voiceless wastes; but a cheerful, busy picture of peasant-life; the strapping wenches at work in the small farm-yards, well-built and frank of face; the men well clad; the children well fed and merry enough. It is a scene that delights the heart of our good friend of Denny-mains. If we had but time, he would fain go in among the tiny farms, and inquire about the rent of the holdings, and the price paid for those picturesque little beasts that the artists are for ever painting—with a louring sky beyond, and a dash of sunlight in front. But our Doctor is obdurate. He will not have Mary Avon walk further; she must return to the yacht.

But on our way back, as she is walking by the side of the road, he suddenly puts his hand on her arm, apparently to stop her. Slight as the touch is, she naturally looks surprised.

"I beg your pardon," he says, hastily, "but I thought you would rather not tread on it——"

He is regarding a weed by the wayside—a thing that looks like a snapdragon of some sort. We did not expect to find a hard-headed man of science betray this trumpery sentiment about a weed.

"I thought you would rather not tread upon it when you knew it was a stranger," he says, in explanation of that rude assault upon her arm. "'That is not an English plant at all; it is the *Mimulus*, its real home is in America."

We began to look with more interest on the audacious small foreigner that had boldly adventured across the seas.

"Oh," she says, looking back along the road, "I hope I have not trampled any of them down."

"Well, it does not *much* matter," he admits, "for the plant is becoming quite common now in parts of the West Highlands; but I thought as it was a stranger, and come all the way across the Atlantic on a voyage of discovery, you would be hospitable. I suppose the Gulf-stream brought the first of them over."

"And if they had any choice in the matter," says Mary Avon, looking down, and speaking with a little self-conscious deliberation, "and if they wanted to be hospitably received, they showed their good sense in coming to the West Highlands."

After that there was a dead silence on the part of Angus Sutherland. But why should he have been embarrassed? There was no compliment levelled at him that he should blush like a schoolboy. It was quite true that Miss Avon's liking—even love—for the West Highlands was becoming very apparent; but Banffshire is not in the West Highlands. What although Angus Sutherland could speak a few words in the Gaelic tongue to an old boatman? He came from Banff. Banffshire is not in the West Highlands.

Then that afternoon at the great castle itself: what have we but a confused recollection of twelfth-century towers; and walls nine feet thick; and ghost-chambers; and a certain fairy-flag, that is called the *Bratach-Sith*; and the wide view over the blue Atlantic; and of a great kindness that made itself visible in the way of hothouse flowers and baskets of fruit, and what not? The portraits, too: the various centuries got mixed up with the old legends, until we did not know in which face to look for some transmitted expression that might tell of the Cave of Uig or the Uamh-na-Ceann. But there was one portrait there, quite modern, and beautiful, that set all the tourist-folk a raving, so lovely were the life-like eyes of it; and the Laird was bold enough to say to the gentle lady who was so good as to be our guide, that it would be one of the greatest happinesses of his life if he might be allowed to ask Mr. Galbraith, the well-known artist of Edinburgh, to select a young painter to come up to Dunvegan and make a copy of this picture for him, Denny-mains. And Dr. Sutherland could scarcely come away from that beautiful face; and our good Queen T. was quite charmed with it; and as for Mary Avon, when one of us regarded her, behold! as she looked up, there was a sort of moisture in the soft black eyes.

What was she thinking of? That it must be a fine thing to be so beautiful a woman, and charm the eyes of all men? But now—now that we had had this singing-bird with us on board the yacht for so long a time—would any one of us have admitted that she was rather plain? It would not have gone well with any one who had ventured to say so to the Laird of Denny-mains, at all events. And as for our sovereign-lady and mistress, these were the lines which she always said described Mary Avon:—

Was never seen thing to be praised derre,[#]
Nor under blacke cloud so bright a sterre,
As she was, as they saiden, every one
That her behelden in her blacke weed;
And yet she stood, full low and still, alone,
Behind all other folk, in little brede,[#]
And nigh the door, ay under shame's drede;
Simple of bearing, debonair of cheer,

With a full surë[#] looking and mannere.
[#] *derre*, dearer.
[#] *in little brede*, without display.
[#] *surë*, frank.

How smart the saloon of the *White Dove* looked that evening at dinner, with those geraniums, and roses, and fuchsias, and what not, set amid the tender green of the maidenhair fern! But all the same there was a serious discussion. Fruit, flowers, vegetables, and fresh milk, however welcome, fill no larder; and Master Fred had returned with the doleful tale that all his endeavours to purchase a sheep at one of the neighbouring farms had been of no avail. Forthwith we resolve to make another effort. Far away, on the outer shores of Dunvegan Loch, we can faintly descry, in the glow of the evening, some crofter's huts on the slopes of the hill. Down with the gig, then, boys; in with the fishing-rods; and away for the distant shores, where haply, some tender ewe-lamb, or brace of quacking duck, or some half-dozen half-starved fowls may be withdrawn from the reluctant tiller of the earth!

It is a beautiful clear evening, with lemon-gold glory in the north-west. And our stout-sinewed Doctor is rowing stroke, and there is a monotonous refrain of

Ho, ro, clansmen!
A long, strong pull together,
Ho, ro, clansmen!

"We must give you a wage as one of the hands, Angus," says Queen T.

"I am paid already," says he. "I would work my passage through for the sketch of Canna that Miss Avon gave me."

"Would you like to ask the other men whether they would take the same payment?" says Miss Avon, in modest depreciation of her powers.

"Do not say anything against the landscape ye gave to Dr. Sutherland," observes the Laird. "No, no; there is great merit in it. I have told ye before I would like to show it to Tom Galbraith before it goes south; I am sure he would approve of it. Indeed, he is jist such a friend of mine that I would take the leeberty of asking him to give it a bit touch here and there—what an experienced artist would see amiss ye know———"

"Mr. Galbraith may be an experienced artist," says our Doctor friend with unnecessary asperity, "but he is not going to touch that picture."

"Ah can tell ye," says the Laird, who is rather hurt by this rejection, "that the advice of Tom Galbraith has been taken by the greatest artists in England. He was up in London last year, and was at the studio of one of the first of the Acadameecians, and that very man was not ashamed to ask the opeenion of Tom Galbraith. And says Tom to him, 'The face is very fine, but the right arm is out of drawing.' You would think that impertinent? The Acadameecian, I can tell you, thought differently. Says he, 'That has been my own opeenion, but no one would ever tell me so; and I would have left it as it is had ye no spoken.'"

"I have no doubt the Academacian who did not know when his picture was out of drawing was quite right to take the advice of Tom Galbraith," says our stroke-oar. "But Tom Galbraith is not going to touch Miss Avon's sketch of Canna———" and here the fierce altercation is stopped, for stroke-oar puts a fresh spurt on, and we hear another sound—

Soon the freshening breeze will blow,
We'll show the snowy canvas on her,
Ho, ro, clansmen!
A long, strong pull together,
Ho, ro, clansmen!

Well, what was the result of our quest? After we had landed Master Fred, and sent him up the hills, and gone off fishing for lithe for an hour or so, we returned to the shore in the gathering dusk. We found our messenger seated on a rock, contentedly singing a Gaelic song, and plucking a couple of fowls which was all the provender he had secured. It was in vain that he tried to cheer us by informing us that the animals in question had cost only sixpence a-piece. We knew that they were not much bigger than thrushes. Awful visions of tinned meats began to rise before us. In gloom we took the steward and the microscopic fowls on board, and set out for the yacht.

But the Laird did not lose his spirits. He declared that self-preservation was the first law of nature, and that, despite the injunctions of the Wild Birds' Protection Act, he would get out his gun and shoot the first brood of "flappers" he saw about those lonely lochs. And he told us such a "good one" about Homesh that we laughed nearly all the way back to the yacht. Provisions? We were independent of provisions! With a handful of rice a day we would cross the Atlantic—we would cross twenty Atlantics—so long as we were to be regaled and cheered by the "good ones" of our friend of Denny-mains.

Dr. Sutherland, too, seemed in no wise depressed by the famine in the land. In the lamp-lit saloon, as we gathered round the table, and cards and things were brought out, and the Laird began to brew his toddy, the young Doctor maintained that no one on land could imagine the snugness of life on board a yacht. And now he had almost forgotten to speak of leaving us; perhaps it was the posting of the paper on Radiolarians, along with other MSS., that had set his mind free. But touching that matter of the Dunvegan post-office: why had he been so particular in asking Mary Avon if she were not expecting letters; and why did he so suddenly grow enthusiastic about the scenery on learning that the young lady, on her travels, was not pestered with correspondence? Miss Avon was not a Cabinet Minister.

CHAPTER XII.
THE OLD SCHOOL AND THE NEW.

The last instructions given to John of Skye that night were large and liberal. At break of day he was to sail for any port he might chance to encounter on the wide seas. So long as Angus Sutherland did not speak of returning, what did it matter to us?—Loch Boisdale, Loch Seaforth, Stornaway, St. Kilda, the North Pole were all the same. It is true that of fresh meat we had on board only two fowls about the size of wrens; but of all varieties of tinned meats and fruit we had an abundant store. And if perchance we were forced to shoot a sheep on the Flannen Islands, would not the foul deed be put down to the discredit of those dastardly Frenchmen? When you rise up as a nation and guillotine all the respectable folk in the country, it is only to be expected of you thereafter that you should go about the seas shooting other people's sheep.

And indeed when we get on deck after breakfast, we find that John of Skye has fulfilled his instructions to the letter; that is to say, he must have started at daybreak to get away so far from Dunvegan and the headlands of Skye. But as for going farther? There is not a speck of cloud in the dome of blue; there is not a ripple on the dazzling sea; there is not a breath of wind to stir the great white sails all aglow in the sunlight; nor is there even enough of the Atlantic swell to move the indolent tiller. How John of Skye has managed to bring us so far on so calm a morning remains a mystery.

"And the glass shows no signs of falling," says our young Doctor quite regretfully: does he long for a hurricane, that so he may exhibit his sailor-like capacities?

But Mary Avon, with a practical air, is arranging her easel on deck, and fixing up a canvas, and getting out the tubes she wants—the while she absently sings to herself something about

Beauty lies
In many eyes,
But love in yours, my Nora Creina.

And what will she attack now? Those long headlands of Skye, dark in shadow, with a glow of sunlight along their summits; or those lonely hills of Uist set far amid the melancholy main; or those vaster and paler mountains of Harris, that rise on the north of the dreaded Sound?

"Well, you *have* courage," says Angus Sutherland, admiringly, "to try to make a picture out of *that*!"

"Oh," she says, modestly, though she is obviously pleased, "that is a pet theory of mine. I try for ordinary every-day effects, without any theatrical business; and if I had only the power to reach them, I know I should surprise people. Because you know most people go through the world with a sort of mist before their eyes; and they are awfully grateful to you when you suddenly clap a pair of spectacles on their nose and make them see things as they are. I cannot do it as yet, you know; but there is no harm in trying."

"I think you do it remarkably well," he says; "but what are you to make of that?—nothing but two great sheets of blue, with a line of bluer hills between?"

But Miss Avon speedily presents us with the desired pair of spectacles. Instead of the cloudless blue day we had imagined it to be, we find that there are low masses of white cloud along the Skye cliffs, and these throw long reflections on the glassy sea, and moreover we begin to perceive that the calm vault around us is not an uninterrupted blue, but melts into a pale green as it nears the eastern horizon. Angus Sutherland leaves the artist to her work. He will not interrupt her by idle talk.

There is no idle talk going forward where the Laird is concerned. He has got hold of an attentive listener in the person of his hostess, who is deep in needlework; and he is expounding to her more clearly than ever the merits of the great Semple case, pointing out more particularly how the charges in the major proposition are borne out by the extracts in the minor. Yes; and he has caught the critics, too, on the hip. What about the discovery of those clever gentlemen that Genesis X. and 10 was incorrect? They thought they were exceedingly smart in proving that the founders of Babel were the descendants, not of Ham, but of Shem. But when the ruins of Babel were examined, what then?

"Why, it was distinctly shown that the founders were the descendants of Ham, after all!" says Denny-mains, triumphantly. "What do ye think of that, Dr. Sutherland?"

Angus Sutherland starts from a reverie: he has not been listening.

"Of what?" he says. "The Semple case?"

"Ay."

"Oh, well," he says, rather carelessly, "all that wrangling is as good an occupation as any other—to keep people from thinking."

The Laird stares, as if he had not heard aright. Angus Sutherland is not aware of having said anything startling. He continues quite innocently—

"Any occupation is valuable enough that diverts the mind—that is why hard work is conducive to complete mental health; it does not matter whether it is grouse-shooting, or commanding an army, or wrangling about major or minor propositions. If a man were continually to be facing the awful mystery of existence—asking the record of the earth and the stars how he came to be here, and getting no answer at all—he must inevitably go mad. The brain could not stand it. If the human race had not busied itself with wars and commerce, and so forth, it must centuries ago have committed suicide. That is the value of hard work—to keep people from thinking of the unknown around them; the more a man is occupied, the happier he is—it does not matter whether he occupies himself with School Boards, or salmon-fishing, or the prosecution of a heretic."

He did not remark the amazed look on the Laird's face, nor yet that Mary Avon had dropped her painting and was listening.

"The fact is," he said, with a smile, "if you are likely to fall to thinking about the real mysteries of existence anywhere, it is among solitudes like these, where you see what a trivial little accident human life is in the history of the earth. You can't think about such things in Regent Street; the cigar-shops, the cabs, the passing people occupy you. But here you are brought back as it were to all sorts of first principles; and commonplaces appear somehow in their original freshness. In Regent Street you no doubt know that life is a strange thing, and that death is a strange thing, because you have been told so, and you believe it, and think no more about it. But here—with the seas and skies round you, and with the silence of the night making you think, you *feel* the strangeness of these things. Now just look over there; the blue sea, and the blue sky, and the hills—it is a curious thing to think that they will be shining there just as they are now—on just such another day as this—and you unable to see them or anything else—passed away like a ghost. And the *White Dove* will be sailing up here; and John will be keeping an eye on Ushinish lighthouse; but your eyes won't be able to see anything——"

"Well, Angus, I do declare," exclaims our sovereign mistress, "you have chosen a comforting thing to talk about this morning. Are we to be always thinking about our coffin?"

"On the contrary," says the young Doctor; "I was only insisting on the wholesomeness of people occupying themselves diligently with some distraction or other, however trivial. And how do you think the Semple case will end, sir?"

But our good friend of Denny-mains was far too deeply shocked and astounded to reply. The great Semple case a trivial thing—a distraction—an occupation to keep people from serious thinking! The public duties, too, of the Commissioner for the Burgh of Strathgovan; were these to be regarded as a mere plaything? The new steam fire-engine was only a toy, then? The proposed new park and the addition to the rates were to be regarded as a piece of amiable diversion?

The Laird knew that Angus Sutherland had not read the *Vestiges of Creation*, and that was a hopeful sign. But, *Vestiges* or no *Vestiges*, what were the young men of the day coming to if their daring speculations led them to regard the most serious and important concerns of life as a pastime? The Commissioners for the Burgh of Strathgoven were but a parcel of children, then, playing on the sea-shore, and unaware of the awful deeps beyond?

"I am looking at these things only as a doctor," says Dr. Sutherland, lightly—seeing that the Laird is too dumbfounded to answer his question, "and I sometimes think a doctor's history of civilisation would be an odd thing, if only you could get at the physiological facts of the case. I should like to know, for example, what Napoleon had for supper on the night before Waterloo. Something indigestible, you may be sure; if his brain had been clear on the 15th, he would have smashed the Allies, and altered modern history. I should have greatly liked, too, to make the acquaintance of the man who first announced his belief that infants dying unbaptised were to suffer eternal torture: I think it must have been his liver. I should like to have examined him."

"I should like to have poisoned him," says Mary Avon, with a flash of anger in the soft eyes.

"Oh, no; the poor wretch was only the victim of some ailment," said our Doctor, charitably. "There must have been something very much the matter with Calvin, too. I know I could have cured Schopenhauer of his pessimism if he had let me put him on a wholesome regimen."

The Laird probably did not know who Schopenhauer was; but the audacity of the new school was altogether too much for him.

"I—I suppose," he said, stammering in his amazement, "ye would have taken Joan of Arc, and treated her as a lunatic?"

"Oh, no; not as a confirmed lunatic," he answered, quite simply. "But the diagnosis of that case is obvious; I think she could have been cured. All that Joanna Southcote wanted was a frank physician."

The Laird rose and went forward to where Mary Avon was standing at her easel. He had had enough. The criticism of landscape painting was more within his compass.

"Very good—very good," says he, as if his whole attention had been occupied by her sketching. "The reflections on the water are just fine. Ye must let me show all your sketches to Tom Galbraith before ye go back to the south."

"I hear you have been talking about the mysteries of existence," she says, with a smile.

"Oh, ay, it is easy to talk," he says, sharply—and not willing to confess that he has been driven away from the field. "I am afraid there is an unsettling tendency among the young men of the present day—a want of respect for things that have been established by the common sense of the world. Not that I am against all innovation. No, no. The world cannot stand still. I myself, now; do ye know that I was among the first in Glasgow to hold that it might be permissible to have an organ to lead the psalmody of a church?"

"Oh, indeed," says she, with much respect.

"That is true. No, no; I am not one of the bigoted. Give me the Essentials, and I do not care if ye put a stone cross on the top of the church. I tell ye that honestly; I would not object even to a cross on the building if all was sound within."

"I am sure you are quite right, sir," says Mary Avon, gently.

"But no tampering with the Essentials. And as for the millinery, and incense, and crucifixes of they poor craytures that have not the courage to go right over to Rome—who stop on this side, and play-act at being Romans—it is seeckening—perfectly seeckening. As for the Romans themselves, I do not condemn them. No, no. If they are in error, I doubt not they believe with a good conscience. And when I am in a foreign town, and one o' their processions of priests and boys comes by, I raise my hat. I do indeed."

"Oh, naturally," says Mary Avon.

"No, no," continues Denny-mains, warmly, "there is none of the bigot about me. There is a minister of the Episcopalian Church that I know; and there is no one more welcome in my house: I ask him to say grace just as I would a minister of my own Church."

"And which is that, sir?" she asked meekly.

The Laird stares at her. Is it possible that she has heard him so elaborately expound the Semple prosecution, and not be aware to what denomination he belongs?

"The Free—the Free Church, of course," he says, with some surprise. "Have ye not seen the *Report of Proceedings* in the Semple case?"

"No, I have not," she answers, timidly. "You have been so kind in explaining it that— that a printed report was quite unnecessary."

"But I will get ye one—I will get ye one directly," says he. "I have several copies in my portmanteau. And ye will see my name in front as one of the elders who considered it fit and proper that a full report should be published, so as to warn the public against these inseedious attacks against our faith. Don't interrupt your work, my lass; but I will get ye the pamphlet; and whenever you want to sit down for a time, ye will find it most interesting reading—most interesting."

And so the worthy Laird goes below to fetch that valued report. And scarcely has he disappeared than a sudden commotion rages over the deck. Behold! a breeze coming swiftly over the sea—ruffling the glassy deep as it approaches! Angus Sutherland jumps to the tiller. The head-sails fill; and the boat begins to move. The lee-sheets are hauled taut; and now the great mainsail is filled too. There is a rippling and hissing of water; and a new stir of life and motion throughout the vessel from stem to stern.

It seems but the beginning of the day now, though it is near lunch-time. Mary Avon puts away her sketch of the dead calm, and sits down just under the lee of the boom, where the cool breeze is blowing along. The Laird, having brought up the pamphlet, is vigorously pacing the deck for his morning exercise; we have all awakened from these idle reveries about the mystery of life.

"Ha, ha," he says, coming aft, "this is fine—this is fine now. Why not give the men a glass of whiskey all round for whistling up such a fine breeze? Do ye think they would object?"

"Better give them a couple of bottles of beer for their dinner," suggests Queen T., who is no lover of whiskey.

But do you think the Laird is to be put off his story by any such suggestion? We can see by his face that he has an anecdote to fire off; is it not apparent that his mention of whiskey was made with a purpose?

"There was a real good one," says he—and the laughter is already twinkling in his eyes, "about the man that was apologising before his family for having been drinking whiskey with some friends. 'Ay,' says he, 'they just held me and forced it down my throat.' Then says his son—a little chap about ten—says he, 'I think I could ha' held ye mysel', feyther'—ho! ho! ho!' says he, 'I think I could ha' held ye mysel', feyther;'" and the Laird laughed, and laughed again, till the tears came into his eyes. We could see that he was still internally laughing at that good one when we went below for luncheon.

At luncheon, too, the Laird quite made up his feud with Angus Sutherland, for he had a great many other good ones to tell about whiskey and whiskey drinking; and he liked a sympathetic audience. But this general merriment was suddenly dashed by an ominous suggestion coming from our young Doctor. Why, he asked, should we go on fighting against these northerly winds? Why not turn and run before them?

"Then you want to leave us, Angus," said his hostess reproachfully.

"Oh, no," he said, and with some colour in his face. "I don't want to go, but I fear I must very soon now. However, I did not make that suggestion on my own account; if I were pressed for time, I could get somewhere where I could catch the *Clansman*."

Mary Avon looked down, saying nothing.

"You would not leave the ship like that," says his hostess. "You would not run away, surely? Rather than that we will turn at once. Where are we now?"

"If the breeze lasts, we will get over to Uist, to Loch na Maddy, this evening, but you must not think of altering your plans on my account. I made the suggestion because of what Captain John was saying."

"Very well," says our Admiral of the Fleet, taking no heed of properly constituted authority. "Suppose we set out on our return voyage to-morrow morning, going round the other side of Skye for a change. But you know, Angus, it is not fair of you to run away when you say yourself there is nothing particular calls you to London."

"Oh," says he, "I am not going to London just yet. I am going to Banff, to see my father. There is an uncle of mine, too, on a visit to the manse."

"Then you will be coming south again?"

"Yes."

"Then why not come another cruise with us on your way back?"

It was not like this hard-headed young Doctor to appear so embarrassed.

"That is what I should like very much myself," he stammered, "if—if I were not in the way of your other arrangements."

"We shall make no other arrangements," says the other definitely. "Now that is a promise, mind. No drawing back. Mary will put it down in writing, and hold you to it."

Mary Avon had not looked up all this time.

"You should not press Dr. Sutherland too much," she says shyly; "perhaps he has other friends he would like to see before leaving Scotland."

The hypocrite! Did she want to make Angus Sutherland burst a blood-vessel in protesting that of all the excursions he had made in his life this would be to him for ever the most memorable; and that a repetition or extension of it was a delight in the future almost too great to think of? However, she seemed pleased that he spoke so warmly, and she did not attempt to contradict him. If he had really enjoyed all this rambling idleness, it would no doubt the better fit him for his work in the great capital.

We beat in to Loch na Maddy—that is, the Lake of the Dogs—in the quiet evening; and the rather commonplace low-lying hills, and the plain houses of the remote little village, looked beautiful enough under the glow of the western skies. And we went ashore, and walked inland for a space, through an intricate network of lagoons inbranching from the sea; and we saw the trout leaping and making circles on the gold-red pools, and watched the herons rising from their fishing and winging their slow flight across the silent lakes.

And it was a beautiful night, too, and we had a little singing on deck. Perhaps there was an under-current of regret in the knowledge that now—for this voyage, at least—we had touched our farthest point. To-morrow we were to set out again for the south.

CHAPTER XIII.
FERDINAND AND MIRANDA.

The wind was laughing at Angus Sutherland. All the time we had been sailing north it had blown from the north; how that we turned our faces eastward, it wheeled round to the east, as if it would imprison him for ever in this floating home.

"*You would fain get away*"—this was the mocking sound that one of us seemed to hear in those light airs of the morning that blew along the white canvas—"*the world calls; ambition, fame, the eagerness of rivalry, the spell that science throws over her disciples, all these are powerful, and they draw you, and you would fain get away. But the hand of the wind is uplifted against you; you may fret as you will, but you are not round Ru Hunish yet!*"

And perhaps the imaginative small creature who heard these strange things in the light breeze against which we were fighting our way across the Minch may have been forming her own plans. Angus Sutherland, she used often to say, wanted humanising. He was too proud and scornful in the pride of his knowledge; the gentle hand of a woman was needed to lead him into more tractable ways. And then this Mary Avon, with her dexterous, nimble woman's wit, and her indomitable courage, and her life and spirit, and abounding cheerfulness; would she not be a splendid companion for him during his long and hard struggle? This born match-maker had long ago thrown away any notion about the Laird transferring our singing-bird to Denny-mains. She had almost forgotten about the project of bringing Howard Smith, the Laird's nephew, and half-compelling him to marry Mary Avon: that was preposterous on the face of it. But she had grown accustomed, during those long days of tranquil idleness, to see our young Doctor and Mary Avon together, cut off from all the distractions of the world, a new Paul and Virginia. Why—she may have asked herself—should not these two solitary waifs, thus thrown by chance together on the wide ocean of existence, why should they not cling to each other and strengthen each other in the coming days of trial and storm? The strange, pathetic, phantasmal farce of life is brief; they cannot seize it and hold it, and shape it to their own ends; they know not whence it comes, or whither it goes; but while the brief, strange thing lasts, they can grasp each other's hand, and make sure—amid all the unknown things around them, the mountains, and the wide seas, and the stars—of some common, humble, human sympathy. It is so natural to grasp the hand of another in the presence of something vast and unknown.

The rest of us, at all events, have no time for such vague dreams and reveries. There is no idleness on board the *White Dove* out here on the shining deep. Dr. Sutherland has rigged up for himself a sort of gymnasium by putting a rope across the shrouds to the peak halyards; and on this rather elastic cross-bar he is taking his morning exercise by going through a series of performances, no doubt picked up in Germany. Miss Avon is busy with a sketch of the long headland running out to Vaternish Point; though, indeed, this smooth Atlantic roll makes it difficult for her to keep her feet, and introduces a certain amount of haphazard into her handiwork. The Laird has brought on deck a formidable portfolio of papers, no doubt relating to the public affairs of Strathgovan; and has put on his gold spectacles; and has got his pencil in hand. Master Fred is re-arranging the cabins; the mistress of the yacht is looking after her flowers. And then is heard the voice of John of Skye—"*Stand by, boys!*" and "*Bout ship!*" and the helm goes down, and the jib and foresail flutter and tear at the blocks and sheets, and then the sails gently fill, and the *White Dove* is away on another tack.

"Well, I give in," says Mary Avon, at last, as a heavier lurch than usual threatens to throw her and her easel together into the scuppers. "It *is* no use."

"I thought you never gave in, Mary," says our Admiral, whose head has appeared again at the top of the companion-stairs.

"I wonder who could paint like this," says Miss Avon, indignantly. And indeed she is trussed up like a fowl, with one arm round one of the gig davits.

"Turner was lashed to the mast of a vessel in order to see a storm," says Queen T.

"But not to paint," retorts the other. "Besides, I am not Turner. Besides, I am tired."

By this time, of course, Angus Sutherland has come to her help; and removes her easel and what not for her; and fetches her a deck-chair.

"Would you like to play chess?" says he.

"Oh, yes," she answers dutifully, "if you think the pieces will stay on the board."

"Draughts will be safer," says he, and therewith he plunges below, and fetches up the squared board.

And so, on this beautiful summer day, with the shining seas around them, and a cool breeze tempering the heat of the sun, Ferdinand and Miranda set to work. And it was a pretty sight to see them—her soft dark eyes so full of an anxious care to acquit herself well; his robust, hard, fresh-coloured face full of a sort of good-natured forbearance. But nevertheless it was a strange game. All Scotchmen are supposed to play draughts; and one brought up in a manse is almost of necessity a good player. But one astonished onlooker began to perceive that, whereas Mary Avon played but indifferently, her opponent played with a blindness that was quite remarkable. She had a very pretty, small, white hand; was he looking at that that he did not, on one occasion, see how he could have taken three pieces and crowned his man all at one fell swoop? And then is it considered incumbent on a draught-player to inform his opponent of what would be a better move on the part of the latter? However that may be, true it is that, by dint of much advice, opportune blindness, and atrocious bad play, the Doctor managed to get the game ended in a draw.

"Dear me," said Mary Avon, "I never thought I should have had a chance. The Scotch are such good draught-players."

"But you play remarkably well," said he—and there was no blush of shame on his face.

Draughts and luncheon carry us on to the afternoon; and still the light breeze holds out; and we get nearer and nearer to the most northerly points of Skye. And as the evening draws on, we can now make out the hilly line of Ross-shire—a pale rose-colour in the far east; and nearer at hand is the Skye coast, with the warm sunlight touching on the ruins of Duntulme, where Donald Gorm Mor fed his imprisoned nephew on salt beef, and then lowered to him an empty cup—mocking him before he died; and then in the west the mountains of Harris, a dark purple against the clear lemon-golden glow. But as night draws on, behold! the wind dies away altogether; and we lie becalmed on a lilac-and-silver sea, with some rocky islands over there grown into a strange intense green in the clear twilight.

Down with the gig, then, John of Skye!—and hurry in all our rods, and lines, and the occult entrapping inventions of our patriarch of Denny-mains. We have no scruple about leaving the yacht in mid-ocean, in charge of the steward only. The clear twilight shines in the sky; there is not a ripple on the sea; only the long Atlantic swell that we can hear breaking far away on the rocks. And surely such calms are infrequent in the Minch; and surely these lonely rocks can have been visited but seldom by passing voyagers?

Yet the great rollers—as we near the forbidding shores—break with an ominous thunder on the projecting points and reefs. The Doctor insists on getting closer and closer—he knows where the big lithe are likely to be found—and the men, although they keep a watchful eye about them, obey. And then—it is Mary Avon who first calls out—and behold! her rod is suddenly dragged down—the point is hauled below the water—agony and alarm are on her face.

"Here—take it—take it!" she calls out. "The rod will be broken."

"Not a bit," the Doctor calls out. "Give him the butt hard! Never mind the rod! Haul away!"

And indeed by this time everybody was alternately calling and hauling; and John of Skye, attending to the rods of the two ladies, had scarcely time to disengage the big fish, and smooth the flies again; and the Laird was declaring that these lithe fight as hard as a twenty-pound salmon. What did we care about those needles and points of black rock that every two or three seconds showed their teeth through the breaking white surf?

"Keep her close in, boys!" Angus Sutherland cried. "We shall have a fine pickling to-morrow."

Then one fish, stronger or bigger than his fellows, pulls the rod clean out of Mary Avon's hands.

"Well, I have done it this time," she says.

"Not a bit!" her companion cries. "Up all lines! Back now, lads—gently!"

And as the stern of the boat is shoved over the great glassy billows, behold! a thin dark line occasionally visible—the end of the lost rod! Then there is a swoop on the part of our Doctor; he has both his hands on the butt; there elapses a minute or two of fighting between man and fish; and then we can see below the boat the wan gleam of the captured animal as it comes to the surface in slow circles. Hurrah! a seven-pounder! John of Skye chuckles to himself as he grasps the big lithe.

"Oh, ay!" he says, "the young leddy knows ferry well when to throw away the rod. It is a gran' good thing to throw away the rod when there will be a big fish. Ay, ay, it iss a good fish."

But the brutes that fought hardest of all were the dog-fish—the snakes of the sea; and there was a sort of holy Archangelic joy on the face of John of Skye when he seized a lump of stick to fell these hideous creatures before flinging them back into the water again. And yet why should they have been killed on account of their snake-like eyes and their cruel mouth? The human race did not rise and extirpate Frederick Smethurst because he was ill-favoured.

By half-past ten we had secured a good cargo of fish; and then we set out for the yacht. The clear twilight was still shining above the Harris hills; but there was a dusky shadow along the Outer Hebrides, where the orange ray of Scalpa light was shining; and there was dusk in the south, so that the yacht had become invisible altogether. It was a long pull back; for the *White Dove* had been carried far by the ebb tide. When we found her, she looked like a tall grey ghost in the gathering darkness; and no light had as yet been put up; but all the same we had a laughing welcome from Master Fred, who was glad to have the fresh fish wherewith to supplement our frugal meals.

Then the next morning—when we got up and looked around—we were in the same place! And the glass would not fall; and the blue skies kept blue; and we had to encounter still another day of dreamy idleness.

"The weather is conspiring against you, Angus," our sovereign lady said, with a smile. "And you know you cannot run away from the yacht: it would be so cowardly to take the steamer."

"Well, indeed," said he, "it is the first time in my life that I have found absolute idleness enjoyable; and I am not so very anxious it should end. Somehow, though, I fear we are too well off. When we get back to the region of letters and telegrams, don't you think we shall have to pay for all this selfish happiness?"

"Then why should we go back?" she says lightly. "Why not make a compact to forsake the world altogether, and live all our life on board the *White Dove*?"

Somehow, his eyes wandered to Mary Avon; and he said—rather absently—

"I, for one, should like it well enough; if it were only possible."

"No, no," says the Laird, brusquely, "that will no do at all. It was never intended that people should go and live for themselves like that. Ye have your duties to the nation and to the laws that protect ye. When I left Denny-mains I told my brother Commissioners that what I could do when I was away to further the business of the Burgh I would do; and I have entered most minutely into several matters of great importance. And that is why I am anxious to get to Portree. I expect most important letters there."

Portree! Our whereabouts on the chart last night was marked between 45 and 46 fathoms W.S.W. from some nameless rocks; and here, as far as we can make out, we are still between these mystical numbers. What can we do but chat, and read, and play draughts, and twirl round a rope, and ascend to the cross-trees to look out for a breeze, and watch and listen to the animal-life around us?

"I do think," says Mary Avon to her hostess, "the calling of those divers is the softest and most musical sound I ever heard; perhaps because it is associated with so many beautiful places. Just fancy, now, if you were suddenly to hear a diver symphony beginning in an opera—if all the falsetto recitative and the blare of the trumpets were to stop—and if you were to hear the violins and flutes beginning, quite low and soft, a diver symphony, would you not think of the Hebrides, and the *White Dove*, and the long summer days? In the winter, you know, in London, I fancy we should go once or twice to see *that* opera!"

"I have never been to an opera," remarks the Laird, quite impervious to Mary Avon's tender enthusiasm. "I am told it is a fantastic exhibeetion."

One incident of that day was the appearance of a new monster of the deep, which approached quite close to the hull of the *White Dove*. Leaning over the rail we could see him clearly in the clear water—a beautiful, golden, submarine insect, with a conical body like that of a land-spider, and six or eight slender legs, by the incurving of which he slowly propelled himself through the water. As we were perfectly convinced that no one had ever been in such dead calms in the Minch before, and had lain for twenty-four hours in the neighbourhood of 45 and 46, we took it for granted that this was a new animal. In the temporary absence of our F.R.S., the Laird was bold enough to name it the *Arachne Mary-Avonensis*; but did not seek to capture it. It went on its golden way.

But we were not to linger for ever in these northern seas, surrounded by perpetual summer calms—however beautiful the prospect might be to a young man fallen away, for the moment, from his high ambitions. Whatever summons from the far world might be awaiting us at Portree was soon to be served upon us. In the afternoon a slight breeze sprung up that gently carried us away past Ru Hunish, and round by Eilean Trodda, and down by Altavaig. The grey-green basaltic cliffs of the Skye coast were now in shadow; but the strong sunlight beat on the grassy ledges above; and there was a distant roar of water along the rocks. This other throbbing sound, too: surely that must be some steamer far away on the other side of Rona?

The sunset deepened. Darker and darker grew the shadows in the great mountains above us. We heard the sea along the solitary shores.

The stars came out in the twilight: they seemed clearest just over the black mountains. In the silence there was the sound of a waterfall somewhere—in among those dark cliffs. Then our side-lights were put up; and we sate on deck; and Mary Avon, nestling close to her friend, was persuaded to sing for her

Yestreen the Queen had four Maries

—just as if she had never heard the song before. The hours went by; Angus Sutherland was talking in a slow, earnest, desultory fashion; and surely he must have been conscious that one heart there at least was eagerly and silently listening to him. The dawn was near at hand when finally we consented to go below.

What time of the morning was it that we heard John of Skye call out "*Six or seven fathoms 'll do?*" We knew at least that we had got into harbour; and that the first golden glow of the daybreak was streaming through the skylights of the saloon. We had returned from the wilds to the claims and the cares of civilisation; if there was any message to us, for good or for evil, from the distant world we had left for so long, it was now waiting for us on shore.

CHAPTER XIV.
EVIL TIDINGS.

We had indeed returned to the world: the first thing we saw on entering the saloon in the morning was a number of letters—actual letters, that had come through a post-office—lying on the breakfast-table. We stared at these strange things. Our good Queen T. was the first to approach them. She took them up as if she expected they would bite her.

"Oh, Mary," she says, "there is not one for you—not one."

Angus Sutherland glanced quickly at the girl. But there was not the least trace of disappointment on her face. On the contrary, she said, with a cheerful indifference—

"So much the better. They only bother people."

But of course they had to be opened and read—even the bulky parcel from Strathgovan. The only bit of intelligence that came from that quarter was to the effect that Tom Galbraith had been jilted by his lady-love; but as the rumour, it appeared, was in circulation among the Glasgow artists, the Laird instantly and indignantly refused to believe it. Envy is the meanest of the passions; and we knew that the Glasgow artists could scarcely sleep in their bed at night for thinking of the great fame of Mr. Galbraith of Edinburgh. However, amid all these letters one of us stumbled upon one little item that certainly concerned us. It was a clipping from the advertisement column of a newspaper. It was inclosed, without word or comment, by a friend in London who knew that we were slightly acquainted, perforce, with Mr. Frederick Smethurst. And it appeared that that gentleman, having got into difficulties with his creditors, had taken himself off, in a surreptitious and evil manner, insomuch that this newspaper clipping was nothing more nor less than a hue and cry after the fraudulent bankrupt. That letter and its startling inclosure were quickly whipped into the pocket of the lady to whom they had been sent.

By great good luck Mary Avon was the first to go on deck. She was anxious to see this new harbour into which we had got. And then, with considerable dismay on her face, our sovereign mistress showed us this ugly thing. She was much excited. It was so shameful of him to bring this disgrace on Mary Avon! What would the poor girl say? And this gentle lady would not for worlds have her told while she was with us—until at least we got back to some more definite channel of information. She was, indeed, greatly distressed.

But we had to order her to dismiss these idle troubles. We formed ourselves into a committee on the spot; and this committee unanimously, if somewhat prematurely, and recklessly, resolved—

First, that it was not of the slightest consequence to us or any human creature where Mr. Frederick Smethurst was, or what he might do with himself.

Secondly, that if Mr. Frederick Smethurst were to put a string and a stone round his neck and betake himself to the bottom of the sea, he would earn our gratitude and in some measure atone for his previous conduct.

Thirdly, that nothing at all about the matter should be said to Mary Avon: if the man had escaped, there might probably be an end of the whole business.

To these resolutions, carried swiftly and unanimously, Angus Sutherland added a sort of desultory rider, to the effect that moral or immoral qualities do sometimes reveal themselves in the face. He was also of opinion that spare persons were more easy of detection in this manner. He gave an instance of a well-known character in London—a most promising ruffian who had run through the whole gamut of discreditable offences. Why was there no record of this brave career written in the man's face? Because nature had obliterated the lines in fat. When a man attains to the dimensions and appearance of a scrofulous toad swollen to the size of an ox, moral and mental traces get rubbed out. Therefore, contended our F.R.S., all persons who set out on a career of villany, and don't want to be found out, should eat fat-producing foods. Potatoes and sugar he especially mentioned as being calculated to conceal crime.

However, we had to banish Frederick Smethurst and his evil deeds from our minds; for the yacht from end to end was in a bustle of commotion about our going ashore; and as for us—why, we meant to run riot in all the wonders and delights of civilisation. Innumerable fowls, tons of potatoes and cabbage and lettuce, fresh butter, new loaves, new milk: there was no end to the visions that rose before the excited brain of our chief commissariat officer. And when the Laird, in the act of stepping, with much dignity, into the gig, expressed his firm conviction that somewhere or other we should stumble upon a Glasgow newspaper not more than a week old, so that he might show us the reports of the meetings of the Strathgovan Commissioners, we knew of no further luxury that the mind could desire.

And as we were being rowed ashore, we could not fail to be struck by the extraordinary abundance of life and business and activity in the world. Portree, with its wooded crags and white houses shining in the sun, seemed a large and populous city. The smooth waters of the bay were crowded with craft of every description; and the boats of the yachts were coming and going with so many people on board of them that we were quite stared out of countenance. And then, when we landed, and walked up the quay, and ascended the hill into the town, we regarded the signs over the shop-doors with the same curiosity that regards the commonest features of a foreign street. There was a peculiarity about Portree, however, that is not met with in continental capitals. We felt that the ground swayed lightly under our feet. Perhaps these were the last oscillations of the great volcanic disturbance that shot the black Coolins into the sky.

Then the shops: such displays of beautiful things, in silk, and wool, and cunning woodwork; human ingenuity declaring itself in a thousand ways, and appealing to our purses. Our purses, to tell the truth, were gaping. A craving for purchase possessed us. But, after all, the Laird could not buy servant girls' scarves as a present for Mary Avon; and Angus Sutherland did not need a second waterproof coat; and though we reached the telegraph office, there would have been a certain monotony in spending innumerable shillings on unnecessary telegrams, even though we might be rejoicing in one of the highest conveniences of civilisation. The plain truth must be told. Our purchases were limited to some tobacco and a box or two of paper collars for the men; to one or two shilling novels; and a flask of eau-de-Cologne. We did not half avail ourselves of all the luxuries spread out so temptingly before us.

"Do you think the men will have the water on board yet?" Mary Avon says, as we walk back. "I do not at all like being on land. The sun scorches so, and the air is stifling."

"In my opeenion," says the Laird, "the authorities of Portree are deserving of great credit for having fixed up the apparatus to let boats get water on board at the quay. It was a public-spirited project—it was that. And I do not suppose that any one grumbles at having to pay a shilling for the privilege. It is a legeetimate tax. I am sure it would have been a long time or we could have got such a thing at Strathgovan, if there was need for it there; ye would scarcely believe it, ma'am, what a spirit of opposition there is among some o' the Commissioners to any improvement, ye would not believe it."

"Indeed," she says, in innocent wonder; she quite sympathises with this public-spirited reformer.

"Ay, it's true. Mind ye, I am a Conservative myself; I will have nothing to do with Radicals and their Republics; no, no, but a wise Conservative knows how to march with the age. Take my own poseetion: for example, as soon as I saw that the steam fire-engine was a necessity, I withdrew my opposition at once. I am very thankful to you, ma'am, for having given me an opportunity of carefully considering the question. I will never forget our trip round Mull. Dear me! it is warm the day," added the Laird, as he raised his broad felt hat, and wiped his face with his voluminous silk handkerchief.

Here come two pedestrians—good-looking young lads of an obviously English type—and faultlessly equipped from head to heel. They look neither to the left nor right; on they go manfully through the dust, the sun scorching their faces; there must be a trifle of heat under these knapsacks. Well, we wish them fine weather and whole heels. It is not the way some of us would like to pass a holiday. For what is this that Miss Avon is singing lightly to herself as she walks carelessly on, occasionally pausing to look in at a shop—

And often have we seamen heard how men are killed or undone,
By overturns of carriages, and thieves, and fires in London.

Here she turns aside to caress a small terrier; but the animal, mistaking her intention, barks furiously, and retreats, growling and ferocious, into the shop. Miss Avon is not disturbed. She walks on, and completes her nautical ballad—all for her own benefit—

We've heard what risk all landsmen run, from noblemen to tailors,
So, Billy, let's thank Providence that you and I are sailors!

"What on earth is that, Mary?" her friend behind asks.

The girl stops with a surprised look, as if she had scarcely been listening to herself; then she says lightly:—

"Oh, don't you know the sailor's song—I forget what they call it:—

A strong sou-wester's blowing, Billy, can't you hear it roar now,
Lord help 'em, how I pities all unhappy folks on shore now.

"You have become a thorough sailor, Miss Avon," says Angus Sutherland, who has overheard the last quotation.

"I—I like it better—I am more interested," she says, timidly, "since you were so kind as to show me the working of the ship."

"Indeed," says he, "I wish you would take command of her, and order her present captain below. Don't you see how tired his eyes are becoming? He won't take his turn of sleep like the others; he has been scarcely off the deck night or day since we left Canna; and I find it is no use remonstrating with him. He is too anxious; and he fancies I am in a hurry to get back; and these continual calms prevent his getting on. Now the whole difficulty would be solved, if you let me go back by the steamer; then you could lie at Portree here for a night or two, and let him have some proper rest."

"I do believe, Angus," says his hostess, laughing in her gentle way, "that you threaten to leave us just to see how anxious we are to keep you."

"My position as ship's doctor," he retorts, "is compromised. If Captain John falls ill on my hands whom am I to blame but myself?"

"I am quite sure I can get him to go below," says Mary Avon, with decision—"quite sure of it. That is, especially," she adds, rather shyly, "if you will take his place. I know he would place more dependence on you than on any of the men."

This is a very pretty compliment to pay to one who is rather proud of his nautical knowledge.

"Well," he says, laughing, "the responsibility must rest on you. Order him below, to-night, and see whether he obeys. If we don't get to a proper anchorage, we will manage to sail the yacht somehow among us—you being captain, Miss Avon."

"If I am captain," she says, lightly—though she turns away her head somewhat, "I shall forbid your deserting the ship."

"So long as you are captain, you need not fear that," he answers. Surely he could say no less.

But it was still John of Skye who was skipper when, on getting under way, we nearly met with a serious accident. Fresh water and all provisions having been got on board, we weighed anchor only to find the breeze die wholly down. Then the dingay was got out to tow the yacht away from the sheltered harbour; and our young Doctor, always anxious for hard work, must needs jump in to join in this service. But the little boat had been straining at the cable for scarcely five minutes when a squall of wind came over from the north-west and suddenly filled the sails. "Look out there, boys!" called Captain John, for we were running full down on the dingay. "Let go the rope! Let go!" he shouted: but they would not let go, as the dingay came sweeping by. In fact, she caught the yacht just below the quarter, and seemed to disappear altogether. Mary Avon uttered one brief cry; and then stood pale—clasping one of the ropes—not daring to look. And John of Skye uttered some exclamation in the Gaelic; and jumped on to the taffrail. But the next thing we saw, just above the taffrail, was the red and shining and laughing face of Angus Sutherland, who was hoisting himself up by means of the mizen boom; and directly afterwards appeared the scarlet cap of Hector of Moidart. It was upon this latter culprit that the full force of John of Skye's wrath was expended.

"Why did you not let go the rope when I wass call to you?"

"It is all right, and if I wass put into the water, I have been in the water before," was the philosophic reply.

And now it was, as we drew away from Portree, that Captain Mary Avon endeavoured to assume supreme command and would have the deposed skipper go below and sleep. John of Skye was very obedient, but he said:—"Oh, ay. I will get plenty of sleep. But that hill there, that is Ben Inivaig; and there is not any hill in the West Highlands so bad for squalls as that hill. By and by I will get plenty of sleep."

Ben Inivaig let us go past its great, gloomy, forbidding shoulders and cliffs without visiting us with anything worse than a few variable puffs; and we got well down into the Raasay Narrows. What a picture of still summer loveliness was around us!—the rippling blue seas, the green shores, and far over these the black peaks of the Coolins now taking a purple tint in the glow of the afternoon. The shallow Sound of Scalpa we did not venture to attack, especially as it was now low water; we went outside Scalpa, by the rocks of Skier Dearg. And still John of Skye evaded, with a gentle Highland courtesy, the orders of the captain. The silver bell of Master Fred summoned us below for dinner, and still John of Skye was gently obdurate.

"Now, John," says Mary Avon, seriously, to him, "you want to make me angry."

"Oh, no, mem; I not think that," says he, deprecatingly.

"Then why won't you go and have some sleep? Do you want to be ill?"

"Oh, there iss plenty of sleep," says he. "Maybe we will get to Kyle Akin to-night; and there will be plenty of sleep for us."

"But I am asking you as a favour to go and get some sleep *now*. Surely the men can take charge of the yacht!"

"Oh, yes, oh, yes!" says John of Skye. "They can do that ferry well."

And then he paused—for he was great friends with this young lady, and did not like to disoblige her.

"You will be having your dinner now. After the dinner, if Mr. Sutherland himself will be on deck, I will go below and turn in for a time."

"Of course Dr. Sutherland will be on deck," says the new captain, promptly; and she was so sure of one member of her crew that she added, "and he will not leave the tiller for a moment until you come to relieve him."

Perhaps it was this promise—perhaps it was the wonderful beauty of the evening—that made us hurry over dinner. Then we went on deck again; and our young Doctor, having got all his bearings and directions clear in his head, took the tiller, and John of Skye at length succumbed to the authority of Commander Avon and disappeared into the forecastle.

The splendour of colour around us on that still evening!—away in the west the sea of a pale yellow green, with each ripple a flash of rose-flame, and over there in the south the great mountains of Skye—the Coolins, Blaven, and Ben-na-Cailleach—become of a plum-purple in the clear and cloudless sky. Angus Sutherland was at the tiller contemplatively smoking an almost black meerschaum; the Laird was discoursing to us about the extraordinary pith and conciseness of the Scotch phrases in the Northumbrian Psalter; while ever and anon a certain young lady, linked arm-in-arm with her friend, would break the silence with some aimless fragment of ballad or old-world air.

And still we glided onwards in the beautiful evening; and now ahead of us in the dusk of the evening, the red star of Kyle Akin lighthouse steadily gleamed. We might get to anchor, after all, without awaking John of Skye.

"In weather like this," remarked our sovereign lady, "in the gathering darkness, John might keep asleep for fifty years."

"Like Rip Van Winkle," said the Laird, proud of his erudition. "That is a wonderful story that Washington Irving wrote—a verra fine story."

"Washington Irving!—the story is as old as the Coolins," says Dr. Sutherland.

The Laird stared as if he had been Rip Van Winkle himself: was he for ever to be checkmated by the encyclopædic knowledge of Young England—or Young Scotland rather—and that knowledge only the gatherings and sweepings of musty books that anybody with a parrot-like habit might acquire?

"Why, surely you know that the legend belongs to that common stock of legends that go through all literatures?" says our young Doctor. "I have no doubt the Hindoos have their Epimenides; and that Peter Klaus turns up somewhere or other in the Gaelic stories. However, that is of little importance; it is of importance that Captain John should get some sleep. Hector, come here!"

There was a brief consultation about the length of anchor-chain wanted for the little harbour opposite Kyle Akin; Hector's instructions were on no account to disturb John of Skye. But no sooner had they set about getting the chain on deck than another figure appeared, black among the rigging; and there was a well-known voice heard forward. Then Captain John came aft, and, despite all remonstrances, would relieve his substitute. Rip Van Winkle's sleep had lasted about an hour and a half.

And now we steal by the black shores; and that solitary red star comes nearer and nearer in the dusk; and at length we can make out two or three other paler lights close down by the water. Behold! the yellow ports of a steam-yacht at anchor; we know, as our own anchor goes rattling out in the dark, that we shall have at least one neighbour and companion through the still watches of the night.

CHAPTER XV.
TEMPTATION.

But the night, according to John of Skye's chronology, lasts only until the tide turns or until a breeze springs up. Long before the wan glare in the east has arisen to touch the highest peaks of the Coolins, we hear the tread of the men on deck getting the yacht under way. And then there is a shuffling noise in Angus Sutherland's cabin; and we guess that he is stealthily dressing in the dark. Is he anxious to behold the wonders of daybreak in the beautiful Loch Alsh, or is he bound to take his share in the sailing of the ship? Less perturbed spirits sink back again into sleep, and contentedly let the *White Dove* go on her own way through the expanding blue-grey light of the dawn.

Hours afterwards there is a strident shouting down the companion-way; everybody is summoned on deck to watch the yacht shoot the Narrows of Kyle Rhea. And the Laird is the first to express his surprise: are these the dreaded Narrows that have caused Captain John to start before daybreak so as to shoot them with the tide? All around is a dream of summer beauty and quiet. A more perfect picture of peace and loveliness could not be imagined than the green crags of the mainland, and the vast hills of Skye, and this placid channel between shining in the fair light of the morning. The only thing we notice is that on the glassy green of the water—this reflected, deep, almost opaque green is not unlike the colour of Niagara below the Falls—there are smooth circular lines here and there; and now and again the bows of the *White Dove* slowly swerve away from her course as if in obedience to some unseen and mysterious pressure. There is not a breath of wind; and it needs all the pulling of the two men out there in the dingay and all the watchful steering of Captain John to keep her head straight. Then a light breeze comes along the great gully; the red-capped men are summoned on board; the dingay is left astern; the danger of being caught in an eddy and swirled ashore is over and gone.

Suddenly the yacht stops as if she had run against a wall. Then, just as she recovers, there is an extraordinary hissing and roaring in the dead silence around us, and close by the yacht we find a great circle of boiling and foaming water, forced up from below and overlapping itself in ever-increasing folds. And then, on the perfectly glassy sea, another and another of those boiling and hissing circles appears, until there is a low rumbling in the summer air like the breaking of distant waves. And the yacht—the wind having again died down—is curiously compelled one way and then another, insomuch that John of Skye quickly orders the men out in the dingay again; and once more the long cable is tugging at her bows.

"It seems to me," says Dr. Sutherland to our skipper, "that we are in the middle of about a thousand whirlpools."

"Oh, it iss ferry quate this morning," says Captain John, with a shrewd smile. "It iss not often so quate as this. Ay, it iss sometimes ferry bad here—quite so bad as Corrievreckan; and when the flood-tide is rinnin, it will be rinnin like—shist like a race-horse."

However, by dint of much hard pulling, and judicious steering, we manage to keep the *White Dove* pretty well in mid-current; and only once—and that but for a second or two—get caught in one of those eddies circling in to the shore. We pass the white ferry-house; a slight breeze carries us by the green shores and woods of Glenelg; we open out the wider sea between Isle Ornsay and Loch Hourn; and then a silver tinkle tells us breakfast is ready.

That long, beautiful, calm summer day: Ferdinand and Miranda playing draughts on deck—he having rigged up an umbrella to shelter her from the hot sun; the Laird busy with papers referring to the Strathgovan Public Park; the hostess of these people overhauling the stores and meditating on something recondite for dinner. At last the Doctor fairly burst out a-laughing.

"Well," said he, "I have been in many a yacht; but never yet in one where everybody on board was anxiously waiting for the glass to fall."

His hostess laughed too.

"When you come south again," she said, "we may be able to give you a touch of something different. I think that, even with all your love of gales, a few days of the equinoctials would quite satisfy you."

"The equinoctials!" he said, with a surprised look.

"Yes," said she boldly. "Why not have a good holiday while you are about it? And a yachting trip is nothing without a fight with the equinoctials. Oh, you have no idea how splendidly the *White Dove* behaves!"

"I should like to try her," he said, with a quick delight; but directly afterwards he ruefully shook his head. "No, no," said he, "such a tremendous spell of idleness is not for me. I have not earned the right to it yet. Twenty years hence I may be able to have three months' continued yachting in the West Highlands."

"If I were you," retorted this small person, with a practical air, "I would take it when I could get it. What do you know about twenty years hence?—you may be physician to the Emperor of China. And you have worked very hard; and you ought to take as long a holiday as you can get."

"I am sure," says Mary Avon very timidly, "that is very wise advice."

"In the meantime," says he, cheerfully, "I am not physician to the Emperor of China, but to the passengers and crew of the *White Dove*. The passengers don't do me the honour of consulting me; but I am going to prescribe for the crew on my own responsibility. All I want is, that I shall have the assistance of Miss Avon in making them take the dose."

Miss Avon looked up inquiringly with the soft black eyes of her.

"Nobody has any control over them but herself—they are like refractory children. Now," said he, rather more seriously, "this night-and-day work is telling on the men. Another week of it and you would see *Insomnia* written in large letters on their eyes. I want you, Miss Avon, to get Captain John and the men to have a complete night's rest to-night—a sound night's sleep from the time we finish dinner till daybreak. We can take charge of the yacht."

Miss Avon promptly rose to her feet.

"John!" she called.

The big brown-bearded skipper from Skye came aft—putting his pipe in his waistcoat-pocket the while.

"John," she said, "I want you to do me a favour now. You and the men have not been having enough sleep lately. You must all go below to-night as soon as we come up from dinner; and you must have a good sleep till daybreak. The gentlemen will take charge of the yacht."

It was in vain that John of Skye protested he was not tired. It was in vain that he assured her that, if a good breeze sprung up, we might get right back to Castle Osprey by the next morning.

"Why, you know very well," she said, "this calm weather means to last for ever."

"Oh, no! I not think that, mem," said John of Skye, smiling.

"At all events we shall be sailing all night; and that is what I want you to do, as a favour to me."

Indeed, our skipper found it was of no use to refuse. The young lady was peremptory. And so, having settled that matter, she sate down to her draught-board again.

But it was the Laird she was playing with now. And this was a remarkable circumstance about the game: when Angus Sutherland played with Denny-mains, the latter was hopelessly and invariably beaten; and when Denny-mains in his turn played with Mary Avon, he was relentlessly and triumphantly the victor; but when Angus Sutherland played with Miss Avon, she, somehow or other, generally managed to secure two out of three games. It was a puzzling triangular duel: the chief feature of it was the splendid joy of the Laird when he had conquered the English young lady. He rubbed his hands, he chuckled, he laughed—just as if he had been repeating one of his own "good ones."

However, at luncheon the Laird was much more serious; for he was showing to us how remiss the Government was in not taking up the great solan question. He had a newspaper cutting which gave in figures—in rows of figures—the probable number of millions of herrings destroyed every year by the solan-geese. The injuries done to the herring-fisheries of this country, he proved to us, was enormous. If a solan is known to eat on an average fifty herrings a day, just think of the millions on millions of fish that must go to feed those nests on the Bass Rock! The Laird waxed quite eloquent about it. The human race were dearer to him far than any gannet or family of gannets.

"What I wonder at is this," said our young Doctor with a curious grim smile, that we had learned to know, coming over his face, "that the solan, with that extraordinary supply of phosphorus to the brain, should have gone on remaining only a bird, and a very ordinary bird, too. Its brain-power should have been developed; it should be able to speak by this time. In fact, there ought to be solan schoolboards and parochial boards on the Bass Rock; and commissioners appointed to inquire whether the building of nests might not be conducted on more scientific principles. When I was a boy—I am sorry to say—I used often to catch a solan by floating out a piece of wood with a dead herring on it: a wise bird, with its brain full of phosphorus, ought to have known that it would break its head when it swooped down on a piece of wood."

The Laird sate in dignified silence. There was something occult and uncanny about many of this young man's sayings—they savoured too much of the dangerous and unsettling tendencies of these modern days. Besides, he did not see what good could come of likening a lot of solan-geese to the Commissioners of the Burgh of Strathgovan. His remarks on the herring-fisheries had been practical and intelligible; they had given no occasion for jibes.

We were suddenly startled by the rattling out of the anchor-chain. What could it mean?—were we caught in an eddy? There was a scurrying up on deck, only to find that, having drifted so far south with the tide, and the tide beginning to turn, John of Skye proposed to secure what advantage we had gained by coming to anchor. There was a sort of shamed laughter over this business. Was the noble *White Dove* only a river barge, then, that she was thus dependent on the tides for her progress? But it was no use either to laugh or to grumble; two of us proposed to row the Laird away to certain distant islands that lie off the shore north of the mouth of Loch Hourn; and for amusement's sake we took some towels with us.

Look now how this long and shapely gig cuts the blue water. The Laird is very dignified in the stern, with the tiller-ropes in his hand; he keeps a straight course enough—though he is mostly looking over the side. And, indeed, this is a perfect wonder-hall over which we are making our way—the water so clear that we notice the fish darting here and there among the great brown blades of the tangle and the long green sea-grass. Then there are stretches of yellow sand, with shells and star-fish shining far below. The sun burns on our hands; there is a dead stillness of heat; the measured splash of the oars startles the sea-birds in there among the rocks.

Send the biorlinn on careering,
Cheerily and all together,
Ho, ro, clansmen!
A long, strong pull together!
Ho, ro, clansmen!

Look out for the shallows, most dignified of coxswains: what if we were to imbed her bows in the silver sand?—

Another cheer! Our isle appears—
Our biorlinn bears her on the faster!
Ho, ro, clansmen!
A long strong pull together!
Ho, ro, clansmen!

"Hold hard!" calls Denny-mains; and behold! we are in among a network of channels and small islands lying out here in the calm sea; and the birds are wildly calling and screaming and swooping about our heads, indignant at the approach of strangers. What is our first duty, then, in coming to these unknown islands and straits?—why, surely, to name them in the interests of civilisation. And we do so accordingly. Here—let it be for ever known—is John Smith Bay. There, Thorley's Food for Cattle Island. Beyond that, on the south, Brown and Poison's Straits. It is quite true that these islands and bays may have been previously visited; but it was no doubt a long time ago; and the people did not stop to bestow names. The latitude and longitude may be dealt with afterwards; meanwhile the discoverers unanimously resolve that the most beautiful of all the islands shall hereafter, through all time, be known as the Island of Mary Avon.

It was on this island that the Laird achieved his memorable capture of a young sea-bird—a huge creature of unknown species that fluttered and scrambled over bush and over scaur, while Denny-mains, quite forgetting his dignity and the heat of the sun, clambered after it over the rocks. And when he got it in his hands, it lay as one dead. He was sorry. He regarded the newly-fledged thing with compassion; and laid it tenderly down on the grass; and came away down again to the shore. But he had scarcely turned his back when the demon bird got on its legs, and—with a succession of shrill and sarcastic "yawps"—was off and away over the higher ledges. No fasting girl had ever shammed so completely as this scarcely-fledged bird.

We bathed in Brown and Poison's Straits, to the great distress of certain sea-pyots that kept screaming over our heads, resenting the intrusion of the discoverers. But in the midst of it, we were suddenly called to observe a strange darkness on the sea, far away in the north, between Glenelg and Skye. Behold! the long-looked-for wind—a hurricane swooping down from the northern hills! Our toilette on the hot rocks was of brief duration; we jumped into the gig; away we went through the glassy water! It was a race between us and the northerly breeze which should reach the yacht first; and we could see that John of Skye had remarked the coming wind, for the men were hoisting the fore-staysail. The dark blue on the water spreads; the reflections of the hills and the clouds gradually disappear; as we clamber on board the first puffs of the breeze are touching the great sails. The anchor has just been got up; the gig is hoisted to the davits; slack out the main sheet, you shifty Hector, and let the great boom go out! Nor is it any mere squall that has come down from the hills;

but a fine, steady, northerly breeze; and away we go with the white foam in our wake. Farewell to the great mountains over the gloomy Loch Hourn; and to the lighthouse over there at Isle Ornsay; and to the giant shoulders of Ard-na-Glishnich. Are not these the dark green woods of Armadale that we see in the west? And southward, and still southward we go with the running seas and the fresh brisk breeze from the north: who knows where we may not be tonight before Angus Sutherland's watch begins?

There is but one thoughtful face on board. It is that of Mary Avon. For the moment, at least, she seems scarcely to rejoice that we have at last got this grateful wind to bear us away to the south and to Castle Osprey.

CHAPTER XVI.
THROUGH THE DARK.

Ahead she goes! the land she knows!

What though we see a sudden squall come tearing over from the shores of Skye, whitening the waves as it approaches us? The *White Dove* is not afraid of any squall. And there are the green woods of Armadale, dusky under the western glow; and here the sombre heights of Dun Bane; and soon we will open out the great gap of Loch Nevis. We are running with the running waves; a general excitement prevails; even the Laird has dismissed for the moment certain dark suspicions about Frederick Smethurst that have for the last day or two been haunting his mind.

And here is a fine sight!—the great steamer coming down from the north—and the sunset is burning on her red funnels—and behold! she has a line of flags from her stem to her top-masts and down to her stern again. Who is on board?—some great laird, or some gay wedding-party?

"Now is your chance, Angus," says Queen T., almost maliciously, as the steamer slowly gains on us. "If you want to go on at once, I know the captain would stop for a minute and pick you up."

He looked at her for a second in a quick, hurt way; then he saw that she was only laughing at him.

"Oh, no, thank you," he said, blushing like a schoolboy; "unless you want to get rid of me. I have been looking forward to sailing the yacht to-night."

"And—and you said," remarked Miss Avon, rather timidly, "that we should challenge them again after dinner this evening."

This was a pretty combination: "we" referred to Angus Sutherland and herself. Her elders were disrespectfully described as "them." So the younger people had not forgotten how they were beaten by "them" on the previous evening.

Is there a sound of pipes amid the throbbing of the paddles? What a crowd of people swarm to the side of the great vessel! And there is the captain on the paddle-box—out all handkerchiefs to return the innumerable salutations—and good-bye, you brave Glencoe!—you have no need to rob us of any one of our passengers.

Where does the breeze come from on this still evening?—there is not a cloud in the sky, and there is a drowsy haze of heat all along the land. But nevertheless it continues; and, as the *White Dove* cleaves her way through the tumbling sea, we gradually draw on to the Point of Sleat, and open out the great plain of the Atlantic, now a golden green, where the tops of the waves catch the light of the sunset skies. And there, too, are our old friends Haleval and Haskeval; but they are so far away, and set amid such a bewildering light, that the whole island seems to be of a pale transparent rose-purple. And a still stranger thing now attracts the eyes of all on board. The setting sun, as it nears the horizon-line of the sea, appears to be assuming a distinctly oblong shape. It is slowly sinking into a purple haze, and becomes more and more oblong as it nears the sea. There is a call for all the glasses hung up in the companion-way; and now what is it that we find out there by the aid of the various binoculars? Why, apparently, a wall of purple; and there is an oblong hole in it, with a fire of gold light far away on the other side. This apparent golden tunnel through the haze grows redder and more red; it becomes more and more elongated; then it burns a deeper crimson until it is almost a line. The next moment there is a sort of shock to the eyes; for there is a sudden darkness all along the horizon-line: the purple-black Atlantic is barred against that lurid haze low down in the west.

It was a merry enough dinner-party: perhaps it was the consciousness that the *White Dove* was still bowling along that brightened up our spirits, and made the Laird of Dennymains more particularly loquacious. The number of good ones that he told us was quite remarkable—until his laughter might have been heard through the whole ship. And to whom now did he devote the narration of those merry anecdotes—to whom but Miss Mary Avon, who was his ready chorus on all occasions, and who entered with a greater zest than any one into the humours of them. Had she been studying the Lowland dialect, then, that she understood and laughed so lightly and joyously at stories about a thousand years of age?

"Oh, ay," the Laird was saying patronisingly to her, "I see ye can enter into the peculiar humour of our Scotch stories; it is not every English person that can do that. And ye understand the language fine.... Well," he added, with an air of modest apology, "perhaps I do not give the pronunciation as broad as I might. I have got out of the way of talking the provincial Scotch since I was a boy—indeed, ah'm generally taken for an Englishman maself—but I do my best to give ye the speerit of it."

"Oh, I am sure your imitation of the provincial Scotch is most excellent—most excellent—and it adds so much to the humour of the stories," says this disgraceful young hypocrite.

"Oh, ay, oh, ay," says the Laird, greatly delighted. "I will admit that some o' the stories would not have so much humour but for the language. But when ye have both! Did ye ever hear of the laddie who was called in to his porridge by his mother?"

We perceived by the twinkle in the Laird's eyes that a real good one was coming. He looked round to see that we were listening, but it was Mary Avon whom he addressed.

"A grumbling bit laddie—a philosopher, too," said he. "His mother thought he would come in the quicker if he knew there was a fly in the milk. '*Johnny,*' she cried out, '*Johnny, come in to your parritch; there's a flee in the milk.*' '*It'll no droon,*' says he. '*What!*' she says, '*grumblin again? Do ye think there's no enough milk?*' '*Plenty for the parritch,*' says he—*kee! kee! kee!*—sharp, eh, wasn't eh?—'*Plenty for the parritch,*' says he—ha! ha! ho! ho! ho!"—and the Laird slapped his thigh, and chuckled to himself. "Oh, ay, Miss Mary," he added, approvingly, "I see you are beginning to understand the Scotch humour fine."

And if our good friend the Laird had been but twenty years younger—with his battery of irresistible jokes, and his great and obvious affection for this stray guest of ours, to say nothing of his dignity and importance as a Commissioner of Strathgovan? What chance would a poor Scotch student have had, with his test-tubes and his scientific magazines, his restless, audacious speculations and eager ambitions? On the one side, wealth, ease, a pleasant facetiousness, and a comfortable acceptance of the obvious facts of the universe—including water-rates and steam fire-engines; on the other, poverty, unrest, the physical struggle for existence, the mental struggle with the mysteries of life: who could doubt what the choice would be? However, there was no thought of this rivalry now. The Laird had abdicated in favour of his nephew, Howard, about whom he had been speaking a good deal to Mary Avon of late. And Angus—though he was always very kind and timidly attentive to Miss Avon—seemed nevertheless at times almost a little afraid of her; or perhaps it was only a vein of shyness that cropped up from time to time through his hard mental characteristics. In any case, he was at this moment neither the shy lover nor the eager student; he was full of the prospect of having sole command of the ship during a long night on the Atlantic, and he hurried us up on deck after dinner without a word about that return-battle at bezique.

The night had come on apace, though there was still a ruddy mist about the northern skies, behind the dusky purple of the Coolin hills. The stars were out overhead; the air around us was full of the soft cries of the divers; occasionally, amid the lapping of the water, we could hear some whirring by of wings. Then the red port light and the green starboard light were brought up from the forecastle, and fixed in their place; the men went below; Angus Sutherland took the tiller; the Laird kept walking backwards and forwards as a sort of look-out; and the two women were as usual seated on rugs together in some invisible corner—crooning snatches of ballads, or making impertinent remarks about people much wiser and older than themselves.

"Now, Angus," says the voice of one of them—apparently from somewhere about the companion, "show us that you can sail the yacht properly, and we will give you complete command during the equinoctials."

"You speak of the equinoctials," said he, laughing, "as if it was quite settled I should be here in September."

"Why not?" said she, promptly. "Mary is my witness you promised. You wouldn't go and desert two poor lone women?"

"But I have got that most uncomfortable thing, a conscience," he answered; "and I know it would stare at me as if I were mad if I proposed to spend such a long time in idleness. It would be outraging all my theories, besides. You know, for years and years back I have been limiting myself in every way—living, for example, on the smallest allowance of food and drink, and that of the simplest and cheapest—so that if any need arose, I should have no luxurious habits to abandon——"

"But what possible need can there be?" said Mary Avon, warmly.

"Do you expect to spend your life in a jail?" said the other woman.

"No," said he, quite simply. "But I will give you an instance of what a man who devotes himself to his profession may have to do. A friend of mine, who is one of the highest living authorities on *Materia Medica*, refused all invitations for three months, and during the whole of that time lived each day on precisely the same food and drink, weighed out in exact quantities, so as to determine the effect of particular drugs on himself. Well, you know, you should be ready to do that——"

"Oh, how wrong you are!" says Mary Avon, with the same impetuosity. "A man who works as hard as you do should not sacrifice yourself to a theory. And what is it? It is quite foolish!"

"Mary!" her friend says.

"It is," she says, with generous warmth. "It is like a man who goes through life with a coffin on his back, so that he may be ready for death. Don't you think that when death comes it will be time enough to be getting the coffin?"

This was a poser.

"You know quite well," she says, "that when the real occasion offered, like the one you describe, you could deny yourself any luxuries readily enough; why should you do so now?"

At this there was a gentle sound of laughter.

"Luxuries—the luxuries of the *White Dove*!" says her hostess, mindful of tinned meats.

"Yes, indeed," says our young Doctor, though he is laughing too. "There is far too much luxury—the luxury of idleness—on board this yacht to be wholesome for one like me."

"Perhaps you object to the effeminacy of the downy couches and the feather pillows," says his hostess, who is always grumbling about the hardness of the beds.

But it appears that she has made an exceedingly bad shot. The man at the wheel—one can just make out his dark figure against the clear starlit heavens, though occasionally he gets before the yellow light of the binnacle—proceeds to assure her that, of all the luxuries of civilisation, he appreciates most a horse-hair pillow; and that he attributes his sound sleeping on board the yacht to the hardness of the beds. He would rather lay his head on a brick, he says, for a night's rest than sink it in the softest feathers.

"Do you wonder," he says, "that Jacob dreamed of angels when he had a stone for his pillow? I don't. If I wanted to have a pleasant sleep and fine dreams that is the sort of pillow I should have."

Some phrase of this catches the ear of our look-out forward; he instantly comes aft.

"Yes, it is a singular piece of testimony," he says. "There is no doubt of it; I have myself seen the very place."

We were not startled; we knew that the Laird, under the guidance of a well-known Free Church minister, had made a run through Palestine.

"Ay," said he, "the further I went away from my own country the more I saw nothing but decadence and meesery. The poor craytures!—living among ruins, and tombs, and decay, without a trace of public spirit or private energy. The disregard of sanitary laws was something terrible to look at—as bad as their universal beggary. That is what comes of centralisation, of suppressing local government. Would ye believe that there are a lot of silly bodies actually working to get our Burgh of Strathgovan annexed to Glasgow—swallowed up in Glasgow!"

"Impossible!" we exclaim.

"I tell ye it is true. But no, no! We are not ripe yet for those Radical measures. We are constituted under an Act of Parliament. Before the House of Commons would dare to annex the free and flourishing Burgh of Strathgovan to Glasgow, I'm thinking the country far and near would hear something of it!"

Yes; and we think so, too. And we think it would be better if the hamlets and towns of Palestine were governed by men of public spirit like the Commissioners of Strathgovan; then they would be properly looked after. Is there a single steam fire-engine in Jericho?

However, it is late; and presently the women say good-night and retire. And the Laird is persuaded to go below with them also; for how otherwise could he have his final glass of toddy in the saloon? There are but two of us left on deck, in the darkness, under the stars.

It is a beautiful night, with those white and quivering points overhead, and the other white and burning points gleaming on the black waves that whirl by the yacht. Beyond the heaving plain of waters there is nothing visible but the dusky gloom of the Island of Eigg, and away in the south the golden eye of Ardnamurchan lighthouse, for which we are steering. Then the intense silence—broken only when the wind, changing a little, gybes the sails and sends the great boom swinging over on to the lee tackle. It is so still that we are startled by the sudden noise of the blowing of a whale; and it sounds quite close to the yacht, though it is more likely that the animal is miles away.

"She is a wonderful creature—she is indeed," says the man at the wheel; as if every one must necessarily be thinking about the same person.

"Who?"

"Your young English friend. Every minute of her life seems to be an enjoyment to her; she sings just as a bird sings, for her own amusement, and without thinking."

"She can think, too; she is not a fool."

"Though she does not look very strong," continues the young Doctor, "she must have a thoroughly healthy constitution, or how could she have such a happy disposition? She is always contented; she is never put out. If you had only seen her patience and cheerfulness when she was attending that old woman—many a time I regretted it—the case was hopeless—a hired nurse would have done as well."

"Hiring a nurse might not have satisfied the young lady's notions of duty."

"Well, I've seen women in sick-rooms, but never any one like her," said he, and then he added, with a sort of emphatic wonder, "I'm hanged if she did not seem to enjoy that, too! Then you never saw any one so particular about following out instructions."

It is here suggested to our steersman that he himself may be a little too particular about following out instructions. For John of Skye's last counsel was to keep Ardnamurchan light on our port bow. That was all very well when we were off the north of Eigg; but is Dr. Sutherland aware that the south point of Eigg—Eilean-na-Castle—juts pretty far out; and is not that black line of land coming uncommonly close on our starboard bow? With some reluctance our new skipper consents to alter his course by a couple of points; and we bear away down for Ardnamurchan.

And of what did he not talk during the long starlit night—the person who ought to have been lookout sitting contentedly aft, a mute listener?—of the strange fears that must have beset the people who first adventured out to sea; of the vast expenditure of human life that must have been thrown away in the discovery of the most common facts about currents and tides and rocks; and so forth, and so forth. But ever and again his talk returned to Mary Avon.

"What does the Laird mean by his suspicions about her uncle?" he asked on one occasion—just as we had been watching a blue-white bolt flash down through the serene heavens and expire in mid-air.

"Mr. Frederick Smethurst has an ugly face."

"But what does he mean about those relations between the man with the ugly face and his niece?"

"That is idle speculation. Frederick Smethurst was her trustee, and might have done her some mischief—that is, if he is an out-and-out scoundrel; but that is all over. Mary is mistress of her own property now."

Here the boom came slowly swinging over; and presently there were all the sheets of the head-sails to be looked after—tedious work enough for amateurs in the darkness of the night.

Then further silence; and the monotonous rush and murmur of the unseen sea; and the dark topmast describing circles among the stars. We get up one of the glasses to make astronomical observations, but the heaving of the boat somewhat interferes with this quest after knowledge. Whoever wants to have a good idea of forked lightning has only to take up a binocular on board a pitching yacht, and try to fix it on a particular planet.

The calm, solemn night passes slowly; the red and green lights shine on the black rigging; afar in the south burns the guiding star of Ardnamurchan. And we have drawn away from Eigg now, and passed the open sound; and there, beyond the murmuring sea, is the doom of the Island of Muick. All the people below are wrapped in slumber; the cabins are dark; there is only a solitary candle burning in the saloon. It is a strange thing to be responsible for the lives of those sleeping folk—out here on the lone Atlantic, in the stillness of the night.

Our young Doctor bears his responsibility lightly. He has—for a wonder—laid aside his pipe; and he is humming a song that he has heard Mary Avon singing of late—something about

O think na lang, lassie, though I gang awa',
For I'll come and see ye in spite o' them a',

and he is wishing the breeze would blow a bit harder—and wondering whether the wind will die away altogether when we get under the lee of Ardnamurchan Point.

But long before we have got down to Ardnamurchan, there is a pale grey light beginning to tell in the eastern skies; and the stars are growing fainter; and the black line of the land is growing clearer above the wrestling seas. Is it a fancy that the first light airs of the morning are a trifle cold? And then we suddenly see, among the dark rigging forward, one or two black figures; and presently John of Skye comes aft, rubbing his eyes. He has had a good sleep at last.

Go below, then, you stout-sinewed young Doctor; you have had your desire of sailing the *White Dove* through the still watches of the night. And soon you will be asleep, with your head on the hard pillow of that little state-room and though the pillow is not as hard as a stone, still the night and the sea and the stars are quickening to the brain; and who knows that you may not perchance after all dream of angels, or hear some faint singing far away?

* * * * *

There was Mary Beaton—and Mary Seaton——

* * * * *

Or is it only a sound of the waves?

END OF VOL. I.

Printed in Great Britain
by Amazon